Totally Bound Publishing books by Beth D. Carter:

Red Wolves Motorcycle Club
Along Came Merrie

I0570893

Red Wolves Motorcycle
Club

ALONG CAME MERRIE

BETH D. CARTER

Along Came Merrie
ISBN # 978-1-78430-372-3
©Copyright Beth D. Carter 2014
Cover Art by Posh Gosh ©Copyright December 2014
Interior text design by Claire Siemaszkiewicz
Totally Bound Publishing

Published in 2014 by Totally Bound Publishing, Newland House, The Point, Weaver Road, Lincoln, LN6 3QN, United Kingdom.

ALONG CAME MERRIE

Dedication

There are many people I have to acknowledge and thank, because no writer is an island. Sure, we think up the words and the plot then bring it all together, but I couldn't do half of that without some amazing people. This book has gone through a journey and the first person I must start with is my BFF, Lark. She's my go-to gal to let me know if something sucks, and thankfully, she told me this one didn't.

Also to Ashlynn Monroe, who is not only an amazing author but an awesome cheerleader. I'm very lucky to call you a friend. Thank you!

A HUGE thank you to Shannon Vasquez, who took the time to read all four Red Wolves novels to let me know if they all made sense. Shannon, you will never know how much that meant to me.

To C.R. Moss, who taught me a lot on editing techniques…now if only I had a tenth of her talent.

And finally, my deepest appreciation to Totally Bound for saying yes. Faith, you have infinite amounts of patience…you rock.

Prologue

Gray Dog eyed the yuppie man, who stepped gingerly into his domain — neatly trimmed hair, boring tie. The expensive cologne that cut through the stench of cigarettes and stale beer belied the cheap suit. Gray Dog might prefer leather and chains, but he knew an off-the-rack suit when he saw one.

He had to give the guy credit. Walking into a biker bar took a lot of guts. The Demon Devils had a reputation — and it wasn't a good one. As he watched the man walk the gauntlet between bikers, Gray Dog grabbed a beer from the cooler and popped the top.

"Have a seat," he said. Most of the time, a prospect tended the bar, but when his arthritis wasn't acting up, he liked to play bartender. He held up the bottle. "Beer?"

"No, thank you," the man said as he sat on a stool.

Gray Dog shrugged and took a long drink. He downed half of it, burped then wiped the moisture off his mustache and beard.

The man took a thick envelope out of his inner suit pocket and laid it down on the countertop. "I've scraped up the money to buy a partnership into your organization."

Gray Dog chuckled. "Organization? I like that. Unfortunately for you, I don't need a partner." He tapped the envelope. "This simply buys you into my distribution."

The man narrowed his eyes. "I'll be the one providing you the girls."

"Let's get one thing straight," Gray Dog said, his words cold and precise. "Your ability to get us *merchandise* would be valuable, but I don't need you. I have the perfect place to get all the girls I need."

"Us?"

Gray Dog waved his hand. "You'll learn, bit by bit."

The man pursed his lips. "All right. Just so that we're clear—any girl I find and you sell, I get a percentage. Correct?"

"There's a little more to it than that, of course. The girls have to be loners—no family, no friends. No one to come looking. They can't see your face. They must be sedated until they reach their destination—and the Master has final approval."

"The Master?"

Gray Dog shrugged. "Just don't call him narcissistic to his face."

"Whatever. I simply want the money. I don't really care what you call one other."

Tilting the half-full bottle in salute, Gray Dog replied, "Then we have an agreement. You toe the line then everything is kosher. You fuck up one time, I'll kill you myself. Clear?"

Gray Dog held out his hand. The man's gaze flicked down at it. Gray Dog sensed the man thinking that he may have made a deal with Satan incarnate.

"Crystal," the man said and accepted the handshake.

Chapter One

Merrie eased up on the gas when she finally accepted the truth. She was lost. Miles from nowhere, she looked down at her gas tank light flickering dangerously low. She dug around on the passenger seat until she found her phone then illuminated it to check her bars.

Of course. Dead.

Story of her life—dead end jobs, dead end future. She'd been taking care of herself since before she should've and the only job she'd been able to get at age fifteen was working on a dairy farm. It was nice but it didn't pay all that much, and she'd gotten tired of her ass being grabbed each time she came by with the coffee carafe. The idea of moving to Cheyenne had sounded good at the time but now—lost in the middle of Wyoming—somehow it didn't seem all that smart. Why was it that none of the roads had marker signs?

She'd gotten turned around at that last pit stop—that's what had happened. Too many roads branched out for the truckers and she'd become confused about which road she'd been on. She was always doing stupid things like that. How hard was it to follow a road?

Apparently, very hard.

It only added to the melancholy lingering in her soul. She had wanted to start over, begin a new chapter in her life, so she'd donated most of her stuff to charity, keeping only the items that were important. It had depressed the hell out of her when she'd discovered all her worldly possessions had fitted in her trunk. It wasn't as if she'd had a happy childhood full of memorabilia and crap. Hell, she'd barely graduated high school.

A glow in the distant sky lifted her spirits. A glow meant people, civilization. Hopefully it also meant a gas station or maybe someone who had information on how far the next one was—and food would be a plus. She hadn't eaten since the truck stop a few hours ago.

She pressed harder on the gas pedal. The quicker she reached the lights, the quicker she'd get back on the right track. Merrie kept her fingers crossed that she wasn't too far from her destination. Who knew driving could be so exhausting?

Her focus stayed on the lights and, as she grew closer, the shape of a large barn converted into a bar drew closer. Dozens of motorcycles surrounded it, big silver and black monstrosities that pushed a slither of unease down her spine. The only bikers she'd really heard of were the made up ones on television and they were dangerous bad asses. Plus, being a woman had her naturally distrustful of bars. There were too many horror stories where a girl went into a bar never to be seen again, and this one held bikers. She slowed upon noticing an old public telephone booth toward the back of the building. Never mind that it belonged in a museum—relief poured through her. She wouldn't have to go inside to ask for directions. She could simply call the police to help her.

Merrie flicked off her headlights as she pulled into the parking lot then headed around back near the telephone booth. She didn't see anyone, so she turned off her car and opened the door. Getting out, she looked around and took a step toward the call box when she heard a man laugh. She swung around. In the shadows of the building, two men talked and shook hands. They wore leather vests with many patches on them but one of the men had a band of red running along the bottom of his while the other didn't. The second man faced her, the patch on his vest white with a red devil and two Ds on it.

Suddenly, the bearded man who faced her turned his head and looked directly at her. He tapped the other guy on the shoulder and he spun on his heel too. The second biker, his goatee cut close to his chin, glared at her like she was something disgusting on the bottom of his shoe. Seriously creeped out, Merrie debated if she should get back in her car and just leave. The telephone stood only a few feet away. Without knowing where she was, she had no way to judge how far the next gas stop would be. Did she really want to be stuck out in the middle of nowhere? Mind made up, she pushed her misgivings away as she hurried over to the phone.

She picked up the receiver, heard a dial tone and breathed a sigh of relief. It worked! She dug in her jeans pocket for some coins and was just about to put them into the phone, when a hand twisted in her hair and pulled sharply. Needle-like pain pricked her scalp and Merrie raised her hands instinctively, trying to alleviate the throb. The phone receiver fell to dangle at the bottom of the phone box.

"Ouch!"

The man holding her hair jerked her away from the phone booth. He twisted his hand, bringing her head up so she stared into his face. Tears flooded her eyes.

"Who are you?" he demanded.

"Let go of me!" she yelled, trying to free herself. This wasn't the first time she'd dealt with this type of torment. Her mother had liked to hurt her whenever she was in her drunken rages.

The biker backhanded her. White-hot heat exploded in her cheek as the force of the hit spun her around. Dirt filled her mouth as she landed hard on her front and tears filled her eyes when her nerve endings processed the pain. Fear replaced every single coherent thought and instinct in Merrie's mind. She pushed herself up and glanced at the man, holding her hands out in a pleading gesture for him to leave her alone.

"I asked who you are," he said coldly. "I didn't ask for a fucking attitude."

"M-my name is M-Merrie," she whimpered, spitting out dirt and blood. Her teeth had cut the inside of her mouth. "P-please don't hurt me."

"Merrie. Well, Merrie, who were you calling?"

"N-no one," she said.

He grabbed her arm and yanked her up to stand in front of him. He bent her arm behind her until she whimpered and tried to pull away, but his grip was too tight.

"Now why don't I believe you?" He shook her. "Were you calling the club? Are you someone's old lady? Or just a fucking spy?"

"I don't know any club. Please let me go!"

"Who were you calling?" he demanded again. This time he brought his hand back in a fist.

"The police!" she cried, cringing.

He leered in her face. The stale stench of cigarettes and the sour fermentation of beer on his breath activated her gag reflex. But she swallowed down the bile. "I've got the police in my back pocket, you stupid bitch. They can't help you."

"I'm lost," she whispered, closing her eyes. "I swear. I was just calling them because I'm lost!"

"Well, shit," someone else said.

Merrie cracked her eyes open. The other man with the gray beard looked at her with a mixture of pity and resolution. Her heart pounded as fear skyrocketed to terror and she knew her life was in jeopardy. Once again, she tugged her arm, trying to break the tight grip on her wrist.

"You fucked up, Axe," the bearded man said. "And I don't know if she'd have someone come looking for her."

"I'll take care of it," Axe snarled.

"Make sure no one finds her body."

"No!" Merrie screamed. "I won't tell anyone anything. I swear. I-I've never been here. I don't even know where I am. Please don't hurt me. Please!"

"Shut up," Axe snarled. He drew back his fist again and smashed it into her face.

Her vision faded and she gave in to the beckoning darkness.

* * * *

Awareness slowly crept back to Merrie. She snapped her eyes open and found herself in the back seat of her car and with her hands tied in front of her. Pain pulsed through the left side of her face but she bit back a sob. Although she didn't know how long she'd been out of it, she was still alive.

She tried to see who was driving, but could only make out the driver wasn't Axe. The person had long dark hair pulled back into a ponytail and a tattoo of a snake on his arm that wrapped from the wrist up into the sleeve of his white T-shirt. Trying to be as sneaky as possible, she began moving her hands about, testing the bonds tying them together. Whoever had bound her hadn't done a very effective job, probably because they expected her to stay unconscious. The rope was loose and she wiggled her wrists even more, pulling as hard as she could without alerting the driver to her movements. A stinging burn chaffed the skin but she didn't care. If she couldn't get free then she was dead, so she strained and tugged carefully and moments later, she'd freed one hand. A sense of elation jolted through her, pumping up her already high level of adrenaline.

She only had one shot at escaping and she knew it was going to hurt like hell when she fell out of the car. Part of her wanted to stay put and try to reason with the men again, but the common sense part of her said that if she stayed there, she would die. Why they wanted her dead she didn't know, but it didn't matter. No one knew where she was and she had no one to rely on either.

By the sound of the car and the way it rolled along, she estimated they were traveling about sixty miles per hour. She couldn't think about the impact of asphalt against her skin at that speed, because something would most likely break.

It was better than the alternative—death.

In her mind, she ran through the plan. She hooked her foot under the door latch. She'd flip it up, the door would open then she would roll head first out of the car, taking the brunt of the impact to her shoulder.

Merrie took a deep breath and mentally counted, psyching herself up. She could do this. She *could* do this!

One...two...three...

It happened just as she'd imagined it would. The door flew open and she crunched her tummy as she forced herself upward enough to sail out of the back seat. She dimly heard the driver curse as she experienced the sensation of freefalling. Down she fell, but instead of asphalt tearing her up, she landed on compact ground and tumbled through tall weeds. Momentum accelerated her along the steep hill. She couldn't stop herself and tried her damnedest to keep her arms tucked against her sides, but it was almost impossible as instinct made her want to use her arms to slow her wild descent, even as gravity propelled her down the embankment. Her right wrist snapped and unimaginable pain forced a scream from her throat. Just as she thought she'd never stop tumbling, she started sliding in the dirt then finally came to a halt as the ground leveled out. She'd reached the bottom.

Merrie lay there crying. She couldn't seem to move as the planet righted itself and vertigo halted. In so much pain she thought she'd pass out, she cradled her wrist. Shouts snapped her out of her haze and she gingerly sat up, looking at the ridge she'd just tumbled down. The road loomed high and the incline appeared sheer. She couldn't count on those bikers to simply ride on and let her go. Regardless, Merrie knew they would be coming for her—and soon.

Tears coursed down her cheeks as she managed to get to her feet and look around. She'd landed in a ravine and the moonlight highlighted the forest that started at its mouth, so she darted into the black glen. She had no idea what to do other than to run as far as possible. Pain ravaged every inch of her body and she knew her wrist was broken, but she didn't feel any other bones poking out from it or anywhere else and for that, she was grateful.

She pushed onward, deeper and deeper into the woods. The only thought in her mind was to keep moving as the need to survive drove her onward. Many times she stumbled but she got right back up, putting one foot in front of the other.

Soon, she didn't hear any more shouts but she refused to relax. Once daylight hit, her pursuers might be able to track her and if she sat to rest, it was possible she'd never be able to get back up. Of course, she had no idea how they'd track her. Did they have dogs? ATVs? What if they had guns? If so, she needed to disappear before they got her in their sights.

Sometime later, she arrived at a small river. It wasn't wide or deep, but the current moved swiftly. A memory filtered through her mind, a television show where the man had used a river to find a farmhouse after being thrown from his horse and breaking an ankle. Sure, it was a TV show, but it was the only thing her brain locked on.

Merrie walked into the river, gasping at the cold, even though it was mid-June. She'd walk for a time in the water to hide her scent, just in case. She put her broken wrist in the water and the cold eased the pain a bit.

Putting one foot in front of the other became her sole focus—her mantra. She blocked out all the hidden dangers of a thick forest. She didn't worry about bears, or wolves, snakes or bugs. Time had no meaning in her little world. She walked in the river until her teeth began to chatter then she sloshed along the bank, stumbling over rocks and terrain. Once she'd warmed up some from her exertion, she stepped back into the river. On and on she went until the sunrise. As light spilled over the forest, nothing else penetrated except for her mantra to take one more step.

The pain in her wrist had long since elevated into nothingness and a tiny voice warned her that she was going into shock, but she didn't have a clue what to do about it, so she kept going. By the time morning had fully dawned—bringing with it some warmth from the sun—she'd left the river somewhere long ago, although she didn't remember when.

Instead, she found herself delirious and on a dirt road, because she thought she saw a rumbling dragon chasing her down. She took off, trying to move away, yet knowing that she wouldn't be able to outrun the beast. She'd come too far to give up now so she pushed on until her body suddenly gave out and she collapsed.

She tried to cry. However, everything she'd used up everything she had in her. She had no tears left. With her good arm, she tried to propel herself along, dragging her limp, useless body until her strength disappeared and she lay face down in the dirt road. If the dragon was going to kill her, she'd rather not see it coming.

As the world began to tilt and fade, she thought she heard the screech of brakes and the slamming of doors. She heard shouts. Someone touched her, turned her over. She stared up into the blue sky, dotted with clouds and thought how pretty the day seemed.

A man's face came into her line of view—different than the bikers—and wearing a cowboy hat. She met his shocked, concerned eyes. A rational part of her brain told her that the stranger would help her. The fear driving her held fast to her mind and she tried to push him away. It didn't work. Her body no longer cooperated.

"P-please don't hurt...me," she begged in a whisper.

"I'm going to help you," the man told her, his voice deep and soothing.

"I...won't tell...w-what I saw."

"Shh. I'm going to call the police—"

Terror engulfed her. No police! *He* would know! *He* would find her! With her last bit of strength, she grabbed his collar and pulled herself up until she was nose to nose.

"No! He'll find me. He'll kill me. He said...the cops are bad. Please...help me!"

The small tether on consciousness she'd clung to snapped. Once again, darkness claimed her.

Chapter Two

Braden McClintock stared with pity at the bedraggled woman in his arms. Someone had beaten her so badly she was one big bloody bruise. He looked toward the timberline she'd stumbled from and listened, but he didn't hear anything.

As her words played back in his head, it was obvious to Braden that she was running from someone. She'd seen something — something that had put her in danger — and she'd said the cops were dirty. If he took her to the hospital, they'd call the sheriff's office, but she was in need of medical help. He suspected her right wrist was broken, owing to the swelling and discoloration. It was obvious someone had hit her on her left cheek. Numerous cuts and scrapes, some of them deep, crisscrossed her body. Her clothing was torn and wet to the touch, which meant she'd walked in the river at some point. The highway was a couple of miles away and if she'd come from there, that meant she'd walked through wolf-infested woods the whole night.

If she was in trouble… If she'd seen something like she'd indicated, then he couldn't bring attention to her. He pulled his cell phone from his back pocket and hit the first number on the speed dial.

"What's up?" his brother, Leo, asked on the other end.

"I have an emergency," Braden answered without preamble. "I'll meet you at your office."

He disconnected and slipped the phone into the front pocket of his shirt before carefully lifting the battered woman into his arms. Moving quickly, he walked to his truck and opened the back seat's door then slowly slid her in. Once he'd secured her, he hopped behind the wheel and quickly turned around then headed back down the road.

About thirty minutes from the ranch and Leo's office, Braden started glancing behind him at the unconscious woman. It was hard for him to tell what she looked like under the dried blood, dirt and swelling. She didn't have a purse or wallet so he didn't even know her name. He wavered back and forth between taking the woman to the hospital and taking her to Leo. He knew what his brother would say—he'd insist that they drive her to the ER—but her words haunted Braden. *What the hell had happened? What have I seen?*

He was still thinking about what to do when he pulled up to Leo's office.

Braden turned the engine off and hurried to get the woman out. Cradling her, he rushed into the building. Leo had built his practice on a corner of their family's property two years ago when the old town vet had finally retired and let Leo take over his workload. He'd filled it with all the latest and best medical gadgets available. Leo still made house calls, of course, but for the most part, his ass stayed firmly on their land.

Leo was waiting for him in the ER bay and Braden gently laid her on the table. Her head listed to the side, exposing her bruised and battered face, the overhead light making it look ten times worse.

"Who's this?" Leo demanded, looking at the woman on his table. He turned stunned eyes toward Braden.

"I found her on the southern road," Braden told him as he arranged the woman's limbs.

"Braden, she needs a hospital, not a veterinarian!"

"I don't think I can take her there," he said. "I think she's in trouble."

"That's obvious, but I treat animals with four legs, not two."

"No, Leo, I mean it. She was conscious long enough to beg me no police and no hospital. She said *he* would find her and kill her."

"He who?" Leo demanded. "Her boyfriend? Her husband? Her pimp?"

"I don't know."

"Is she dangerous?"

Braden' shot his eyebrows up. "Does she look dangerous?"

"I meant is she involved with dangerous company. Damn it, Braden—"

"Look," he interrupted, waving his arm around. "You can take X-rays, you've got plaster, medicine and you're a fucking doctor. I just have this gut feeling she needs protection. So please, do me this favor."

Leo sighed and rubbed the back of his neck. "All right. But if she's a fugitive or some kind of con artist, I'm calling the cops and kicking your ass. Got it?"

Braden held his hands up in an *I give up and agree* gesture. Leo reached for gloves and slipped them on to begin his examination. He tilted the woman's head this way and that before grabbing a pair of bandage scissors.

"I think she was out in the woods all night," Braden said, as he watched his brother treat her. "Probably went through the river."

"We need to get her on an IV and X-ray that wrist," Leo stated. "Hopefully that's the only broken bone she has. Help me take her clothes off."

Braden grabbed gloves as well and they both slowly cut her clothing away, revealing bruises over most of her body. Purple contusions covered her side, as well as her hips with more mottling down her legs. Leo probed her ribs and listened to her lungs then gestured for Braden to cover her with a blanket.

"Get the saline on that shelf over there to clean up the dried blood," Leo ordered. "Find all the cuts that require stitches."

Braden did as he was told while Leo started an IV drip in her left wrist. As Braden washed her, he realized that the woman was young, probably in her early twenties, with curly brown hair reaching halfway down her back. Of course, leaves and sticks matted her hair, but he'd tackle that job later.

Most of her cuts were minor, needing only antibiotic ointment and Band-Aids. She had only two that seemed deep enough for stitches—one on her thigh and one on her shoulder. He pointed them out to Leo, who left to get a package of suture, gloves and a sterile medical kit. Braden had helped Leo a couple of times in the lab so he snagged some povidone-iodine to clean the area as his brother used a clamp to grab the curved needle which had the thread attached at the tail. Leo sewed with finesse, his concentration focused solely on his work. When he finished, he slipped off his gloves to bandage the two areas, careful of her wrist, before rewrapping her in the blanket.

"Let's X-ray that wrist," Leo said. "I want one of her torso too, although I didn't feel any other broken bones or internal swelling when I palpated. But I must stress that it would be better if she could have a CT scan." Leo glowered at him.

"Noted, Dr. Leo," Braden said as he unhooked the safety from the table wheels. The X-ray machine sat in another room behind protective radiation shielding. They laid a small lead vest around her neck to protect her thyroid then moved behind the protective sheeting as Leo activated the machine, snapping several shots of her hand, followed by a couple of her chest. When they were done, Braden removed the neck shield.

"Well, this is good," Leo said as he looked at the pictures. "No internal bleeding or broken bones that I can see. The break on her radius is clean and the carpus cluster looks fine, which is relief. Of course, I would feel better if a hand surgeon took a look at these."

"Do you know a hand surgeon?"

"No," Leo answered. "But I could call over at Riverton and see if they have one there. I know I'd feel a helluva lot better if I didn't have this on my conscience."

Braden rubbed his jaw, thinking. "No. Not until we talk to her."

"Ah hell, Braden. What's up with this girl? You're such a levelheaded guy and yet you're acting crazy right now. Think!"

"You weren't there, Leo. You didn't hear her pleading with me, scared out of her mind. Since I don't know what she witnessed, I can't take the chance of someone recognizing her if I take her to the hospital. I have to protect her. Now, please…just put a cast on her wrist."

Leo glared at him. "What if I've missed something? What if she needs surgery on her wrist? The decisions we make right now could seriously affect her prognosis."

"I trust you, Leo."

His brother gave a fed-up groan, turned and stormed away.

Braden strode back to the woman and caressed her cheek. Although pale and fragile-looking, she was pretty. Protectiveness surged through him and he touched her curls, letting one swirl around his fingers. He'd only talked to her for a moment, but he couldn't get her terrified expression out of his mind.

"I…won't tell…w-what I saw."

"Shh. I'm going to call the police – "

"No! He'll find me! He'll kill me! He said…the cops are bad. Please…help me!"

Who was this man who had terrified her, beat her black and blue and left her wandering at night in the forest? A lover? A stranger? Whoever he was, it didn't take a genius to figure out she was probably in the wrong place at the wrong time and had witnessed something that put her life in danger. Her escape was a testament to her courage, since she'd spent the night running for her life while in terrible pain.

Yet he knew Leo was right. As he wheeled the table back into the lab, he decided he'd give the unconscious woman two days—unless something medically threatening happened. Later, if she played him or if he sensed she wasn't being truthful, he'd take her in and let the police deal with her.

Chapter Three

Merrie blinked her eyes open, although the lid on her left side barely fluttered. It seemed swollen but as she reached up to touch it, pain flared through her shoulder. She moaned and let her arm drop onto the bed.

"It's going to be okay," a man's soothing voice said.

She flinched in surprise, looking in the direction of the voice. A cowboy leaned on the doorframe. Big and muscular, he sported a pale blue button-up shirt tucked into tight-fitting jeans and boots. He took off his hat as he stepped inside the bedroom, revealing a head full of dark hair threaded with silver and in need of a cut.

Bedroom? Merrie darted her gaze around, taking in the sunny room. A vanity stood in the corner and a mirror showed her a horrifying sight. A bruise marred her usually creamy complexion and there was a cut on her cheek that appeared raw. Now she knew why heat and tightness riddled her face.

But the bigger question was—where the hell was she? The last thing she remembered was being in the woods, terrified out of her mind that she would stumble across Axe or the tattooed man who had driven her car.

"W-where am I?"

"You're on my ranch."

She winced as her chapped lips cracked. She didn't even have enough saliva to wet them with her tongue. Water would be heavenly.

"There's a glass of water on your nightstand," he said, with a nod to her left. "If you don't mind, I'll help you to sit up."

Merrie tried to move herself, which was a stupid thing to do since the small shift sent off an explosion of pain through her whole body. There wasn't one place that didn't hurt, including her hair. She felt as if a truck had run her over then someone had strung her out to dry.

"Okay," she said, biting back a moan.

The cowboy set his hat on the bedpost as he moved to her left side. He slid his big hands slowly under her arms and she rested her one good hand on his shoulders as he gently lifted her into an upright position. She realized she wore a very large T-shirt and nothing else. When he let go, he snatched the pillow and fluffed it before sliding it between her back and the headboard. The whole effort took only a couple of minutes, but sweat broke out on her forehead and Merrie felt as though she'd run a marathon.

"My name is Braden McClintock." He picked up the glass of water and handed it over.

She accepted it gratefully. In a few big gulps, she'd drained the glass.

"More?" he asked.

"I'm okay for now." She closed her eyes for a moment and took in how she felt. Now that she'd rested, the pain had subsided into one big, aching mess. "I'm Merrie. Merrie Christmas Walden."

"Really? That's your name? Were you born on December twenty-fifth or something?"

"No," she said with a sigh. She'd been answering that question all her life. "My mother just liked the holiday."

He offered her a ghost of a smile. "Do you remember what happened to you?"

She glanced at the cast on her right arm. "Yes. Did you take me to the hospital?"

"No, you begged me not to."

Merrie let out a sigh of relief she hadn't realized she'd been holding. "Thank you."

"Are you in trouble? Because you're a mess and I had to fight with my brother about not taking you to the hospital. He's a vet."

"As in the military?"

Braden shook his head. "As in veterinarian. He treated you."

"Oh. Tell him thanks."

Braden gestured to the bed. "May I?"

"Sure."

He sat and stared hard at her, his blue eyes seemingly searching for answers. She didn't know what to tell him or if she should tell him anything at all. Would he be in danger if she explained what had happened to her? Somehow she didn't think he'd let her simply gloss over the details.

"I'm on your ranch?"

"Yes," he said. "Well, mine and my brother's. His name is Leo. He's out on a call right now but he's going to be back soon, wanting answers, so why don't you start with what sort of trouble you're in."

Her gaze fell to the cast on her arm. "I was moving—heading to Cheyenne—and got lost. I've never been very good with navigation. Finally, I decided to stop at this bar I saw and call for directions."

"Route 18?"

"I don't know. I guess it's a biker bar since the parking lot was full of motorcycles."

Braden nodded. "It's the local hangout for the Demon Devils."

Fear shot through her. "Y-you're not part of them, are you?"

"No," he replied.

She relaxed.

"Did they do this to you? Did they...hurt you in other ways?"

She shook her head. "I wasn't raped. I wanted to use the payphone I saw, because my cell was dead. I thought if I called the police, I could get some help or directions."

"Christ," he muttered. "The Demon Devils are an outlaw gang."

"I don't know what that means."

"It means they operate outside of the law and the last thing they'd want is the police showing up on their doorstep. Tell me, Merrie. Tell me everything."

So she did. She probably should've kept quiet since she didn't know if she could fully trust him, but she'd never been the type of person who could keep everything bottled inside. Braden had taken her in, had patched her up, and she was so damn grateful just to be alive that her emotions practically bubbled over.

When she was done with her tale, Braden rubbed the back of his neck as he contemplated her. She didn't know what she'd do if he asked her to leave. She had nothing. She'd left her purse in her car, along with her money, clothes and the rest of her possessions.

"You should talk to the police," he finally said. "I know Givon Halloran, the sheriff. Believe me, he's not part of *that* club."

She widened her eyes in fear and shook her head adamantly. "No, he said the police were their friends. I can't. No, I just can't!"

"Okay, Merrie—"

"I just want to move on and forget this happened!" she continued, as if she hadn't heard him. "I need to get away from here, away from Wyoming. I was moving to the city but I could easily just leave the state."

"Merrie—"

"I'm close, aren't I? I'm close to that bar, right? I walked a long time last night but not far enough. He'll find me!"

Braden placed a comforting hand on her shoulder and she instantly calmed down. He was a big man, tough, with a resolute look about him that made it seem like he would be a mountain to move. Even if it was an illusion, she sensed she was safe with him.

"No one is going to hurt you, Merrie. You begged me to help you and I plan on doing just that. You're pretty messed up and from what I can see, you don't have any ID or... Look, why don't we take one day at time and you work on healing? Let the bruises fade, let the bones in your wrist set then we'll decide what to do next."

She took a deep breath and nodded. He was right. Logically, she knew he was right, but she couldn't seem to completely ignore the fear lurking inside her. Those vicious men were still out there and they were close.

He gave her a small, tentative smile.

Outside, a vehicle pulled up. An engine turned off and the sound of a door snapping shut reached her. A door opened somewhere far away and the sound of boots moving across a floor, the echo coming from below, immediately reached her. She realized she must be in a two-story home. Merrie tensed.

"It's okay," Braden told her. "That will be Leo. He'll want to come and talk to you about your injuries. Okay?"

She nodded again. He rose and picked up his cowboy hat as he walked out of the bedroom. Self-pity washed through her, brought on by helplessness. What was she going to do? Maybe, once she was better, Braden would drive her to Casper or Laramie, somewhere big where the Demon Devils couldn't touch her.

Maybe she should just get out of Wyoming altogether—head to some place like Salt Lake City or Denver. She could disappear in a big city, so as long as she never saw the biker, Axe, again.

* * * *

"How's the Johnston's cow doing?" Braden asked as he descended the stairs.

"Good. The poor thing got tangled up in some barbwire. I hate barbwire." Leo set his bag by the door then strode into the kitchen. He opened the fridge and pulled out a pitcher of iced tea. "How's the patient?"

While Leo poured himself a glass of tea, Braden flopped his hat onto the table. "Awake. Her name is Merrie Walden. I told her you'd be up to see her."

"What the hell happened to her?"

"The Demon Devils."

Leo paused with the glass halfway to his mouth. "Shit."

Braden nodded grimly. "She was lost, stopped to use the phone then some man named Axe attacked her. She jumped from the back seat of her car when they were taking her away, fell down an embankment, which is how she broke her wrist, and got banged up. Then she spent the night fleeing through the woods. She said they were going to kill her."

"She needs to go to the cops," Leo insisted.

"Axe made it sound like they were in his pocket."

"Do you think that could be true? Givon and North are pretty tight."

"Do we want to take that chance?"

Leo frowned, stared at his drink then drank half of the tea before he set the glass on the counter. "Let me go talk to her."

As Leo brushed by him, Braden grabbed his brother's arm. "Be nice to her."

"Of course," Leo grumbled, extracting himself. "I have an excellent bedside manner."

"Yeah, but you can't scratch this patient behind the ear or pat her belly."

Leo grinned and walked to his bag by the front door. He bent and retrieved his stethoscope before heading upstairs.

Merrie glanced up when a small knock sounded. The door was already open and a Native American man stood grinning at her. Even in her battered condition, she realized how handsome he was with short black hair and dark brown eyes.

"Hi. I'm Leo Cloud Dancer."

"You're Braden's brother?"

Leo walked farther into the room and looked at her plastered wrist. "Honorary. His parents took me in and raised me with Braden. Helped get me through school then they co-signed my student loans. They're good people, but they got tired of Wyoming winters so they moved to Florida."

After examining her wrist, he began a check-up that included pupil dilation, counting her pulse and listening to her lungs. When he was done, he draped the stethoscope around his neck and rocked back on his heels to study her.

"I have to be honest, Merrie," he said. "I wanted to take you to the hospital."

"Thank you for not doing that," she replied. "I don't know if that man—Axe—would be scouting the hospitals or if the staff would be obligated to call the police. I just can't trust them after what he said."

He sighed. "All right. As long as nothing goes sour, I won't beat a dead horse."

"Oh, bad pun."

"Sorry." A bit of amusement resided in his tone. "Do you feel up to talking about what you saw?"

"That's just it," she said. "I don't know what I saw. I think that man Axe thought I was someone else and when he realized I wasn't, it was too late. He'd already assaulted me."

"We'll keep you safe here until you get on your feet," he assured her. "I'm at the ranch most days. My practice is only half a mile down the road. Braden is usually in and out, dealing with the horses."

She bit the part of her lip that wasn't sore. "I'm sorry about this, about imposing on you."

"Are you kidding? It was quite interesting treating a two-legged person instead of something with fur."

She chuckled then winced. "Don't make me laugh."

"Then don't talk to Braden," Leo said, immediately losing all levity. "He's the jokester in the family."

Merrie eyed him dubiously. Braden McClintock had seemed more taciturn than funny. Then Leo's lips twitched and she realized he was joking with her, which caused her to chuckle and hold her sides.

"Oh, you're a very bad man for making me laugh," she chastised with a smile.

He patted her hand. "I suspect you're going to be bored, lying in bed. Am I right?"

She nodded. "I'm a doer not a lay-about, although I'm not sure how to help out with this cast. Plus, I'm right-handed, so don't hand me a paring knife or I'm likely to need a whole different kind of bandage."

"I've got an e-reader full of books. You can borrow it. If there's anything you want, just download it."

"What if I download some steamy romance?"

"Who's to say it's not already on there?"

She raised an eyebrow. "Well, Mr. Cloud Dancer, you are definitely not like your brother."

"Thank God," Leo praised, glancing skyward.

She gave another muffled laugh then groaned.

"Sorry. You're very easy to tease."

"Are you flirting with me?"

"Being a vet, I never thought I'd say this to a patient, but I have an ethical responsibility not to flirt with you."

"Yeah, that does sound slightly weird. I was only teasing, you know."

He smiled. "I know. Hey, we can be a couple of teases together, which is good to keep Braden from being too serious. He's only two years older than I am but sometimes he acts like my grandfather. Speaking of family, is there anyone we can call for you?"

She shook her head as her smile immediately slid away. "I don't have anyone anymore. I was actually moving to Cheyenne in hopes of finding a better job."

"What about friends who will worry about you?"

"None. I guess I'm the perfect person to murder—no one to come looking for me." She bit her bottom lip but that didn't do much to quiet her quivering chin. She looked away from his warm brown eyes. "Pretty pathetic, huh?"

He took her left hand in his and rubbed the soft skin on her wrist with his thumb. The contrast between their colorings transfixed her.

"It's okay," he told her. "Merrie, why did these men do this to you?"

"I wish I knew," she whispered. "They were talking about making sure to h-hide my body. And I believed them, Leo. I was so scared."

She struggled to hold back the tears from the terror still lingering inside her. She'd come so close to dying, to vanishing without anyone being the wiser. And the thought of that man, Axe, finding her to finish what he'd started, settled in her soul like a festering wound.

Merrie shifted and winced.

"Would you like some pain medication?" Leo asked. "It'll help you rest and right now you need lots of sleep. That's when your body heals."

"Okay," she whispered.

He let go of her hand, rose and walked out of the bedroom. A few minutes later, he returned with a glass bottle and a new syringe. He opened the syringe package, drew up the medicine then injected it into her arm.

"Rest now." Leo pushed a curl off her forehead.

Soon, lethargy flowed into her veins and she closed her eyes. She let the oblivion of the drug work its magic and succumbed to the peaceful arms of sleep.

Leo couldn't stop staring at her. Merrie Walden wasn't what he had expected, although now that he thought about it, he wasn't quite sure what he *had* been expecting. In the back of his mind, he'd really thought this whole thing had been a scam, sucking Braden into whatever con she was concocting. But there was no denying the anxiety and shock still swimming in her toffee-colored eyes.

She was a strong woman, although he doubted she realized it. Not many people could keep their wits about them long enough to plan an escape or even face the pain she'd known she was going to inflict by jumping out of a speeding car.

Even under her fear, he could see her spunk.

He rose and retraced his steps back downstairs where he slid the used capped needle into his case to dispose of it properly once he got back to his office.

Braden stood at the table bent over a map.

"You were reading my mind," he said, coming to stand next to his brother.

"I'd like a look at the road she was traveling on, see if we can find anything," Braden stated. He circled an area with his index finger. "If we factor in her starting point was the bar and I found her here, not to mention the fact that she walked through the river, I'm thinking she had to jump from the car somewhere around here. Do you think it's okay to leave her alone?"

"I gave her a shot of pain medicine. She's going to be out for a few hours. But just in case, we'll leave her a brief message that we'll be back soon."

Leo could see Braden mulling things over in his mind. He knew his brother didn't want to leave her alone, because Leo didn't want to either. Something about Merrie tugged on his heartstrings. More than just the abuse she'd suffered, Leo felt drawn to her and it made him want to help her, in any capacity.

After a few minutes, Braden gave a nod and Leo picked up the map, folding it so they could see the area Braden had pointed out. He scribbled a quick note and left it on the table. He made sure they'd locked the front door before heading to Braden's truck. He tried to push his worries aside, because no one could trace Merrie Walden to them, even if one of those men had been tracking her through the forest. She hadn't emerged on their property. Braden had been on his way to talk to a neighbor about a few horses and had used the southern road.

This time Braden took the paved main road, which twisted a little out of the way but had an on ramp for Route 18. The bar lay toward the southwest, so Braden turned north and drove slowly. Leo kept his eyes focused on the side of the road, hoping to see anything that might be a clue.

A few minutes later, he pointed. "Look. The shoulder disappears around that curve and gives way to a sheer embankment."

"Merrie said she fell straight down instead of hitting the asphalt."

Braden pulled over, while the road still had a shoulder, and jabbed the hazard lights on before turning off the engine.

"How far do you think we are from the Demon Devil's bar?" Braden asked.

"Uh, fifteen miles? Not quite sure," Leo answered.

They jumped out of the truck and began walking. Route 18 was a two-lane road that occasionally opened up into three so cars could pass slow-moving vehicles. It had once been the only road that linked the small town of Destiny to the bigger city of Cody, but that had changed once the nearby highway had been built. Now Route 18 was used mostly for locals, ranchers, and of course, for the Demon Devil Motorcycle Club that had moved in almost twenty years ago.

"Leo," Braden said, pointing. "Look at the grass. It's been trampled."

Leo bent over to study the tall stalks of weeds and a flattened path down the side.

"That's at least fifty yards down," he muttered.

"Christ," Braden muttered. "She jumped out of a car and rolled down that? How the hell did she survive?"

Leo shook his head in amazement. "And the only bone she broke was her wrist. She's fucking lucky."

"Come on," Braden said. "Let's cruise past the bar, see if we see anything."

Leo wasn't so sure that was a wise decision but he was curious too. They probably wouldn't be so bold as to have her car out where anyone could see it, but stupider things had happened.

Braden stepped on the gas and sometime later, they drove by the Demon Devil's hang out. A mile down the road, Braden made a U-turn in the middle of the road and drove by again, this time a little slower than before. Bikes surrounded the bar and a large sign held a white circle with two black D's in the center with a devil in the background boldly proclaiming ownership to the Demon Devils.

They didn't see a car, so Braden sped up and hurried back to the ranch. Leo was glad. He suddenly didn't want Merrie left alone.

"What do we do now?" he asked.

Braden shook his head. "I don't know."

Chapter Four

When Merrie opened her eyes again, twilight peeked through the window's lace curtains. Her wrist throbbed but the pain was minimal until she moved. Wincing, she took stock of the rest of her body, feeling like one big stubbed toe.

"Be careful," Leo said, as he entered the room. He carried a lap tray that held steaming soup, crackers and a glass of water. "Dinner."

Behind him, Braden followed, minus his hat this time.

She took the glass of water and drank it down thirstily. When she had finished, she handed the empty glass back to Leo.

"Can one of you help me to the bathroom before I eat?"

Braden nodded and stepped forward. Instead of helping her out of bed, he scooped her up and carried her to the hallway bathroom. For a moment, as she clung to his shoulders, her heart fluttered and her breath hitched. Her unexpected attraction toward Braden McClintock unsettled her and she made a conscious effort not to show how she'd reacted to his touch.

"This is an older house, so we only have two bathrooms," he informed her. His gaze fell to her lips and lingered. When he raised his eyes once more, she saw a flash of answering desire before he hid behind his expressionless façade.

"So it's a communal bathroom," she said, breathless.

He nodded. "But Leo and I will share the one downstairs until you —"

"Don't be silly," she said. "Do both of you sleep on the second floor?"

"Yes."

"Then don't let me disrupt your routine. I'm an unwanted guest."

He gently set her down just outside the blue-painted bathroom, but didn't let go of her arms right away. When she glanced up at him curiously, wondering why he still held her upper arm, she saw a fleeting emotion she couldn't identify in his eyes.

"You're not unwanted," he told her. "I'll stay right here and wait till you're done then I'll carry you back."

"You don't have to do that," she said softly.

"Leo and I want you to heal, not because we want you to leave." He traced a finger gently around the cut on her face. Tenderness softened the hard angles of his face.

At his touch, her heart erupted with longing and brought forth a smattering of tears that she quickly hid by nodding and turning away. When she closed the door, she took a moment to breathe deeply and collect herself. She'd never had someone tell her something so sweet, not even her mother. It had made her feel…cared for.

When she finished, she opened the door. Without a word, Braden swung her up in his arms and carried her back to the bedroom. After he propped her up and made her comfortable, Leo set the tray across her lap so she could eat. Both Leo and Braden got chairs to sit next to her.

"We think we found the spot where you jumped out of the car and tumbled down the embankment," Leo said. "You are one lucky woman."

She swallowed a mouthful of soup. Her empty stomach rejoiced at finally having something to fill it.

"We also drove by the Demon Devil's bar but didn't see your car," Braden added.

Anxiety shot through Merrie. "Are you crazy? They're dangerous."

"It's okay," Leo assured her. "We didn't stop, just looked."

"Merrie," Braden said. "I did some research online about motorcycle clubs and the local ones around Destiny. For membership into a club, a person has to go through a trial period for a designated time, usually a year, in which they have to do everything the leader and the other members tell them to do. It's a sort of ritual to show devotion to the gang."

"Okay," she murmured, wondering where the conversation was heading.

"These potential members are called prospects and for an outlaw gang, which is what the Demon Devils are, that usually means something illegal."

"So what you're saying… What *are* you saying?"

"That maybe you were a command to a prospect. A hazing. Or a way to show loyalty."

Merrie thought about last night, thought about what the two men had said. Then she thought about being in her car, how the driver was someone different.

"I don't know," she replied. "Maybe."

"If that's the case," Braden continued. "I'm concerned about the next woman that man, Axe, comes across."

The thought stopped her cold and her spoon clattered back into her bowl. Ice formed in the pit of her stomach.

"I never thought of that," she whispered.

"We want to take photos of you," Leo said, holding up a digital camera. "We want to document all your injuries, just in case."

She looked at both men and nodded. "Okay. I guess you both have seen me naked already."

"In a purely medical way," Leo assured.

She offered him a fleeting smile, although she didn't feel any amusement. "Teasing. Remember?"

He winked at her, which lifted her spirits a tad.

"We also want to call the authorities in Cheyenne," Braden said, after throwing Leo a strange look.

Merrie realized she was having a hard time interpreting the enigmatic Braden McClintock. One minute she melted under his touch and the next he was formal and in control.

"Since there's a possibility the Destiny Sheriff's Department might not be completely trustworthy, we thought the police in a different city might help us out."

"Us?" she whispered. "You can dump me on them, dust your hands of any further involvement. I'd understand, Braden."

He shook his head. "I made a promise to keep you safe and until we figure all this out, Leo and I will take care of you."

Tears gathered in her eyes again and she rapidly blinked them away. This might be one of those psychological problems that arise when a patient starts to develop feelings for her rescuers, but damn if she didn't feel a spark for both men. Gratitude? A big hell yes but also something more, something…tangible.

"Thank you," she said, clearing her throat.

Leo took the tray and set it aside while Braden helped her out of bed once more.

"Can you help me with the T-shirt?" she asked him.

A muscle ticked in his jaw but he only nodded. He grabbed hold of the shirt and carefully took it off her. Both Leo and Braden' narrowed their eyes as they looked at her body. She turned to look in the vanity mirror.

Holy hell, she looked worse than she thought. Her chest, sides and abdomen were one big black and purple bruise. The rounded part of her right shoulder reminded her of a large, black plum. Stitches poked out like railroad ties on her shoulder and thighs. Scabbed abrasions covered the rest of her skin. This time, she couldn't hold back the tears. Leo gently gathered her in his arms and she buried her head in his neck.

"Shh," he soothed. "It's going to be all right. You're okay. You're safe. You hear me, Merrie? You're safe with Braden and me. We're going to protect you."

Even though she was naked, he held her tenderly, gently and made her feel protected and she thanked whatever divine intervention had led her to the doorstep of her guardian angels.

After she'd finally gathered her emotions, she posed for the photos. Leo took them in a way that managed to capture the horror her body had gone through while not showing her breasts or anything below the navel — for which she was grateful.

Braden helped her with the T-shirt then fluffed the pillow against her back as she eased back into bed. Even that little bit of movement exhausted her and she closed her eyes as she relaxed into the comfortable folds of the bed. The coolness of the sheets against her heated and swollen skin brought a measure of relief.

"Do you want some more pain medicine?" Leo asked her.

She cracked an eye to look at him. "I don't want to get addicted to the stuff."

"I think one more dose wouldn't hurt," he assured her. "You need a good night of rest and you'll not be able to do that if you're waking up constantly in pain."

"I slept most of today away. Why am I so sleepy now?"

He patted her hand then held it lightly. "This is normal. Your body uses a lot of energy to heal itself."

"Okay," she said. Truth be told, she desperately wanted to dull the overwhelming ache pulsing through her body. She watched through half-closed eyes as Leo prepared another new syringe, drawing the medicine up through the rubber stopper then easing the needle into her arm. She'd never been a fan of needles or the slight sting as one penetrated her skin, but compared to everything else, she didn't even feel it go in this time.

Braden moved her hair off her shoulder. When she turned her head to look at him, her vision swam. The pain med had already begun to kick in.

"Have a good night," he told her.

She smiled at him as sleep enveloped her.

* * * *

Leo sat down heavily at the kitchen table and scrolled back through the photos he'd just taken of Merrie. They were horrible and his stomach clenched at the thought that the asshole was still out there and could potentially hurt another woman. What type of monster did this?

"You know anyone at the Cheyenne PD?" his brother asked, as he placed the tray containing Merrie's dirty dishes on the counter.

"No," Leo replied. "I don't suppose you do?"

Braden shook his head. "No. I only know Givon and right now we can't exactly trust him. Which sucks."

"I know, but I don't want this character Axe learning that we have Merrie."

"I know." Braden sat across from Leo. A frown furrowed his brow. "We're her only protection."

"I'm glad you found her," Leo said softly, "and I'm glad you brought her to me."

"She's special. A lesser woman might have given up."

"Our job now is to keep her on the mend and keep her safe."

"Agreed."

A deep understanding passed between them, and Leo knew without a doubt Merrie Walden was going to turn their lives completely around.

Chapter Five

Detective Clark Christianson finished off the rest of his coffee before throwing the cup in the nearest trash can. He gave a nod to another passing detective — someone from vice, he thought — but he couldn't remember the guy's name. Really, who the hell cared? He didn't. Not anymore.

He got on the elevator and hit the button to his floor, ignoring the other officers crowding the small enclosure. He only had two more weeks then he could retire with his full pension. It wasn't so much the money but the medical was too good to piss off. Otherwise, he'd say fuck it and head off to go fishing.

As he walked toward his desk, his cell phone rang and he pulled it from the clip and looked at the number. He stopped, double-checked that he was seeing the same number and swore under his breath.

"Why are you calling me at this number?" he snarled.

"We got trouble."

"Fuck, Axe, why do you do this to me? Whatever it is, I can't fucking help you. And don't call me on this number again."

"Wait, Clark! This affects you too. There's a girl out there who can put me in jail. And if I go to jail then they're going to find out about you."

Clark's stomach bottomed out and he glanced around at his coworkers to see if anyone had overheard his brother. He didn't need this fucking shit. Two weeks left and his dumb shit outlaw brother was going fuck everything up.

"Listen to me, you dumb fuck," Clark snapped in as quiet of a voice that he could muster and still show him his anger. "You've screwed up your life and I'll be goddamned if you screw up mine. I have two weeks until I retire."

"And if this girl goes to the cops and identifies me, how's your pension going to hold up under an IAB investigation?"

Clark wished he could reach through the phone and wring his brother's neck. Heartburn clawed in his gut, twisting his insides up. He closed the door to his office to make sure no one could see how weird he was acting. "Who is she?"

"Merrie Walden. She escaped from me but she knows my name and she knows what I look like."

"And what did you do to her?"

"She saw me talking to someone she shouldn't have. I thought she was a spy from North and I... Well—I threatened her."

"You threatened her? Why do I doubt it's that simple?"

Axe sighed. "I might have punched her. And she might have heard me planning on hiding her body."

"Fuck! I hate you, Axe. Do you hear me?"

"Yes, yes. But you've got as much to lose as I do, Clark—at least for two more weeks you do. So find me Merrie Walden."

The line went dead and Clark wanted to smash the device against the wall when sanity prevailed. He'd have a tough time explaining a sudden fit to his boss. His younger brother had always driven him nuts. Axe had changed his name when he'd turned eighteen, said being a 'son of Christ' wasn't helping his outlaw image, then when Clark had decided to go into law enforcement, Clark had been glad to have the so-called skeleton of his brother tucked far away into the closet.

He'd been stupid to assume he could finish out his career clean and simple. Two fucking weeks and his brother was going to screw it all up. Clark ran a hand through his hair as he opened his door, ready to go get some milk. It was the only thing that helped his upset stomach. Great. What a great fucking day this was turning out to be.

"Hey, Clark," his boss said. "We got a strange call from a rancher in Destiny. It was about a woman who was beaten up by a biker."

Clark blinked, unsure if this was a colossal joke or not. He wondered who the hell he'd pissed off to get saddled with this shit.

"Why didn't this rancher call the Destiny sheriff?"

"The guy said the cops up there may be on the take. When you get a moment, will you check it out?"

"Sure," Clark said. "What's the woman's name?"

His Captain looked at his notes. "Merrie. Merrie Walden."

* * * *

The next day Merrie didn't do anything more productive than limp to the bathroom. Her body ached and all she wanted to do was sleep. Braden brought her breakfast and dinner and Leo visited her around lunchtime. They were busy men and she regretted that they had to wait on her and she vowed to get up as soon as possible to figure out some way to pay them back.

Her dreams had been a kaleidoscope of all her terrors, starting with her mother, segueing into the shit-hole she'd lived through, as well as the underlining fear of Axe still out there somewhere, and ending with worst case scenarios of what would happen if he caught her. None of it was pretty. She'd lived an ugly life for the most part but she'd never be one to bemoan the woe-is-me scenario. She'd woken often throughout the night and tried to think of happy things, but she couldn't escape for long. Whenever she'd succumbed to slumber again, *he* was waiting for her.

The third day progressed much like the day before, only she was able to stay awake longer. She read on Leo's e-reader, bypassing the mysteries and thrillers for the classics. The last thing she wanted to read was who-done-its in fiction when her own life was a bit complicated. She'd never been one of those people who could pick up a book and sit just to enjoy reading it. Her life was about work, not about simple pleasures. Back in her hometown, she'd gotten up before dawn to head to her to day job at a dairy farm, helping to monitor the milk-processing machines, and her evenings were spent in the diner, where she served food. She'd been supporting herself before she'd even graduated high school and her Great Uncle Clarence had died, leaving her without family.

When she was seventeen, she'd escaped the system on her word that she'd stay in school and finish her senior year. It'd been tough but she'd done it. Now, six years later, she was once again at a crossroads in her life.

On the dawn of the fourth day, Merrie pulled herself out of bed. She went into the bathroom to use the facilities and managed to wash herself without getting her cast wet. She'd only given herself a sponge bath for two days but her hair had remained dirty, so having a proper shower with clean hair felt like heaven.

Most of her bruises had started to turn an ugly mustard-yellow color while others, the larger ones, were more violet-green. She wrapped the towel around herself and opened the door, only to smack into a very hard chest.

She looked up into Braden's blue eyes staring back at her in consternation.

"You should be in bed," he said.

"I'm feeling better," she announced. "I've gotten a lot of rest and, honestly, I'm starting to feel a little stir-crazy in that bed."

Standing so close to him with his blue eyes studying her intently, Merrie suddenly became aware of how big Braden McClintock actually was. He filled the doorway, shoulder to shoulder. Had he been wearing his hat, he wouldn't have made it through without ducking. His dark locks peppered with silver tumbled about his forehead and she itched to run her fingers through it and straighten out the mess. Lighter lines crinkled from the corner of his eyes, showing off his tan. His face was a bit craggy from the years working in the sun and weather, but handsome in a tough, masculine way.

"You want me to help you to the downstairs living room? We have a TV with satellite, so I'm sure you can find something to watch while I whip us up some breakfast."

"That would be great."

Braden swooped her up in his arms. She gasped at the suddenness and threw her arms around his neck to balance herself.

"I can walk," she protested.

"I don't want you to fall down the stairs."

"I can make it down the stairs just fine. Besides, I need to put a T-shirt on."

He turned toward one of the back bedrooms and entered it, setting her on her feet as he rummaged through a dresser drawer. She realized this was his room and looked around. Stark, white walls. Plain, sensible furniture. One picture of a very old family portrait, showing a teenage Braden and Leo standing next to a sitting man and a woman, hung forlornly on the wall. Merrie assumed they were his parents. She wondered if a quarter would bounce on his tightly made bed. Not a single stitch of discarded clothing lay around.

He handed her a T-shirt and spun around, giving her a little privacy. She dropped the towel and slipped the extra-large shirt over her head. After she tugged it down over her hips, the garment's hem touched her thighs.

"All right," she said.

He turned around and took in her form, his eyes widening a little. For a long moment, they simply stared at one another. Could he hear how her heart thundered in the silence of the room? Surely her heartbeat echoed through the near-empty chamber, pumping an off-kilter rhythm. What was happening to her? She didn't want this attraction, so she broke their locked gazes by bending to pick up the damp cloth. He took a step toward her, so close she could smell him—clean and fresh of the wild outdoors with an underlying hint of male spice. Braden took the towel from her, tossed it on the bed then scooped her back up in his arms to head for the stairway.

Up close and personal, she studied his profile—the hard angles and planes that told of a rugged life. A cowboy lived under the sunshine and in the elements. He'd lived most of his life outside and it wasn't hard to picture him riding a horse across the plains. She liked how he held her, how he cradled her in his arms against his chest, and she had a sudden flash of running her hands over those smooth pectorals. Merrie raised her gaze to his lips and she wondered what they would feel like against hers. Soft? Unyielding? Dominant?

At the bottom of the stairs, he happened to look down at her and froze. She brought her gaze from his mouth up to stare into his crystalline blue eyes. The color rivaled the beautiful Caribbean waters she'd seen in travel magazines.

"Your eyes are gorgeous," she said.

Braden lowered his lashes and didn't acknowledge her compliment as he hurried into the living room and placed her gently on the sofa. When he turned to walk away, she grabbed his hand, reluctant to let him go.

"I'm sorry if I embarrassed you," she said.

"They're just eyes. Yours are…pretty too."

"They're just plain ol' brown."

He shifted closer and stared deeply into them. Merrie's body heated and her heart shifted from beating quickly to full-out hammering.

"No, there are tiny flakes of gold in them," he murmured. "I'd say they're more amber than brown."

She wanted to kiss him. She had no clue when he'd gone from savior to sexy but Braden McClintock was one piece of male who stimulated all her buttons. Just as she moved closer so she could put her mouth on his, he blinked and straightened. He abruptly left her — left the room — leaving her wondering what the hell had just happened. She thought they were about to share a wonderful moment, but obviously, she'd read him wrong.

Story of her life. Always a day late and a dollar short, as her Great Uncle Clarence said. The Walden's had terrible luck, so it shouldn't come as a surprise that she was attracted to a man who didn't seem to want her back. She picked up the remote and began flipping through the channels, trying desperately not to replay the almost kiss in her head.

Chapter Six

Listening to Braden bang around in the kitchen forced her to give up any hope of concentrating on the television. Soon, the aroma of breakfast permeated the air and her stomach rumbled. She'd been on a diet of soft foods such as oatmeal and soup, so when Braden appeared with eggs and toast, Merrie felt as if she'd been shown heaven.

He set the plate on the coffee table. She picked up the toast then bit into it, closing her eyes in pleasure.

"Mmm," she said. "That is so good. Thank you, Braden."

He shrugged. "Just let me know if you start feeling nauseous."

"Aren't you eating with me?"

"Actually, I have to get going," he told her. "I'm meeting with a client to look over some of my horses."

"Oh. Is this a big horse ranch?"

"No, a small one, but it keeps me busy." He gestured to the front door. "Leo is at the clinic. He should be there until lunch or if he gets an emergency call. The ground floor bathroom is under the staircase."

"I'll be fine, Braden," she assured. "I'm sore but there's no longer any sharp pain."

"Good," he murmured. He stared at her for a long moment before he brushed one tanned finger down her bruised cheek. "You're safe here, Merrie."

Her mouth dried up as she stared into his eyes. "I know," she whispered.

Braden gave her one last searing look and withdrew his finger. She keenly felt the loss of his touch. At the doorway, he hesitated before reaching in his back pocket to take out his cell phone. He touched the screen then laid it on the coffee table near the plate.

"I've unlocked it," he told her. "Leo is speed dial number two if you need anything."

"Okay."

The sound of the closing door echoed through the house, or at least it seemed that way to her. Alone for the first time since she'd woken up in the house. Rooted to her spot, she craned her head to listen for the truck engine. Once the rumble faded, a stillness, void of any white noise or hum of nature, hung in the air. The men had explained she'd be safe in their home, but the unpleasant, dead quiet of the house unsettled her, made her imagination want to run to dark corners and reveal the boogeymen waiting for her there.

She rubbed her arms and shook off the imagery. It dawned on her what a long day it would be in the house alone, although it had been an interesting morning. In the few days she'd known Braden McClintock, she'd come to learn he was a stoic man. He rarely smiled and usually only talked when he needed to say something.

He was not the type of man she typically dated. Most of her boyfriends were closer to her own age, fun loving party boys whose brains were located in their pants. It was one of the many reasons why she'd decided to move away. She came from a small town and after dating most of the eligible bachelors, she'd managed to get a reputation and the last thing she wanted was to be compared to her mother.

She'd gotten sick of boys but Braden was not a boy — he was all man. Of course, there was the fact that he'd rescued her, which left her confused. Was she attracted to him because he'd helped her, taken her in and protected her? Was she transferring her gratitude into something more? She didn't want to be one of those silly girls who convinced herself she was falling in love when it was a simple case of hero worship.

More than a little unsettled with her thoughts, she turned on the television back on and watched a movie while she ate her breakfast and pushed Braden firmly to the back of her mind.

* * * *

After a couple of hours, her bladder needed relieving. Carefully, she limped to the small restroom under the stairs. She heard the front door open then Leo called her name. She hurriedly finished her business, washed her useable hand, and when she opened the door, found him looming in the doorway, one fist raised to knock. Startled, Merrie gave a high-pitched squeal. When Leo reached out to steady her, she ended up tripping into his arms.

For a minute, she just stared into his eyes and he gazed back. Her heart beat frantically from the fright he'd given her but it soon gave way to something different. Awareness sizzled along her nerve endings as if she'd gotten too close to a live wire. His gaze flicked briefly to her mouth and, briefly, hunger flared in the dark depths of his eyes.

Then he dropped his arms from around her and stepped back. He didn't say anything as he spun on his heel and walked away. She took a deep, steadying breath, turned off the light and ambled back to the couch. Leo was in the kitchen. Sounds of his puttering around as he made lunch reached her. She picked up his e-reader and opened it to browse his books. Suddenly he set down two plates, each one with a sandwich and potato chips. He disappeared back into the kitchen and when he returned, he carried two cans of soda. He handed her one and she took it with a grateful smile.

"Thank you for lunch," she said.

He shrugged. "I don't like eating alone. I'm a boring self-conversationalist."

She chuckled. "Well, I've had nothing but daytime talk shows to sit through, so even if you spouted out mathematical equations for the next hour, I'd much prefer your company."

"Um, thanks?"

They ate their lunches in comfortable companionship. She couldn't help but sneak peeks at him, admiring his sharp profile. The heritage of his ancestors resided in his features, softened only slightly by a different way of life. The raven hue of his hair shimmered with blue in the sunlight. His eyes were so dark it was hard to tell the irises from the pupils. He caught her studying him.

"Why are you staring at me?"

"You're a very handsome man," she answered, deciding to be straightforward with him. "You and

Braden both are. Why aren't you two married? Or at least involved with someone."

"Braden was married a long time ago," he replied. "It didn't work out. As for me, I've spent most of my life getting to where I am today. I wasn't a disciplined student so it took me a long time to accomplish my goals. I never had time to pursue a relationship."

"How old are you?"

"I'm thirty-eight. Braden is forty. How old are you?"

"I've just turned twenty-three. But I've decided that I'll stop aging when I hit twenty-nine."

"Oh, yeah? Good luck with that."

"Thanks," she replied breezily. "So Braden told me this is a small horse ranch."

"Keeps him busy. Used to be a cattle ranch years ago, when his great granddad first started it. Braden's father, Clip, began the transition to horses."

"And how did you come live with them?"

"My father used to work for Braden's dad." He took a long drink of his soda. "I would come with him and hang out with the horses, and I was good with them. When my father was killed in a car accident, Clip went to my mother and offered to raise me. I have seven other siblings, all younger, so she agreed."

"Ouch. That must have stung."

"No, not really. I understood but I also didn't mind because I liked it here. Braden was a great older brother."

"I'm envious," she murmured.

He raised his eyebrows.

"Oh, I don't mean because of your loss," she hurried to explain. "I meant having something there for you, someone to care for you. My mother was too much into her drugs to give a shit about me, and I never knew who my dad was."

Concern and sympathy flooded his eyes. "That's rough."

"That's life," she corrected. "I've never been one of those 'oh, woe is me' kind of girls."

Admiration replaced the sympathy in his expression. "So you're headed to Cheyenne for fun and action?"

"No," she said emphatically. "I was headed there to try to find a better job, a better life."

"What skills do you have?"

"Well, I know my way around a dairy farm but I want get away from that type of employment. I can type and I'm good with people, so figured I could find an office job."

He pursed his lips. "Well, if you want, my office assistant is on a two-week vacation and I've been swamped answering the phones as well as trying to deal with patients."

She widened her eyes. "I could help you!"

She saw his gaze flicker over her bruised cheek. After four days, the swelling had abated and the bruise had changed from dark hues into a faint yellow. She covered the blemish with her hand.

"Makeup will hide this," she said. "Please. I've never been a sit around type of person. I like working."

He thought for a moment longer before slowly nodding. "All right, but you'll let me buy you some clothes. As sexy as you look in that T-shirt, I don't think I'd be able to concentrate if that's all you wore each day."

As his words sank into her brain, her mouth fell open. He just said she was sexy. *Really?*

He cleared his throat. "I shouldn't have said that. Never mind, Merrie, I —"

"Please," she interrupted. "It's okay. I...I think you and Braden are sexy as well. It's normal to feel that way. I'm walking around half-naked and you're both my knights in shining armor."

A frown briefly touched between his eyes before smoothing out. Whatever he'd been thinking — or maybe about to say — vanished as he stood, picking up her plate.

"Are you finished?" he asked.

She nodded, suddenly confused. What had she said to make him shut down? He returned to the kitchen where he clinked the dishes as he put them in the sink. Then he turned back to face her.

"I have a few house calls to make," he said. "Let me deal with them then afterward we'll head into town. You can borrow some of my sweats for now."

"Leo, are you okay?"

"Of course. Why wouldn't I be?"

"We were having a nice conversation and suddenly you just...turned cool."

He sighed and ran a hand through his hair. "Forgive me, Merrie. It's just me acting stupid. Rest for now and I'll be back in a couple of hours."

Leo turned to leave but before he closed the door behind him, he shot her a wink, leaving her feeling very confused. Not too long ago she'd wanted very much to kiss Braden and now she longed for the same with Leo. What kind of woman did that make her? Sure, she'd had lustful feelings for different men at the same time, but she'd never had the thought or desire to act upon those feelings. She'd never considered herself a girl who'd enjoy a threesome, but today she would've gladly succumbed to her desire for both men.

She hadn't had the best role model growing up, since her mother often traded sexual favors for her fix. At sixteen, she'd lost her virginity in the back of a car to the football jock, not really caring that it was something precious. In her book, if she didn't give it away it would be forced from her so why not make it halfway pleasant? Over the years, sex had been more for the man she'd been with than for any personal enjoyment. But with Braden and Leo, she was actually aroused. Excited. Maybe it was because she knew they cared about her. That alone was stimulating enough. There was something sexy about having an emotional tie to someone, although she still wasn't sure what to think about herself now.

Chapter Seven

A couple of hours later, Leo returned from his house calls. He headed upstairs and a few minutes after, she heard the shower start. When he came back downstairs, his damp hair lay plastered to his skull. Merrie had taken it upon herself to find the sweats he'd mentioned earlier. They were big on her, as was the T-shirt, and she felt slightly self-conscious not wearing a bra. But there was a sense of excitement that she'd soon have clothes that would fit her again. Truly, it was the little things in life.

Braden still hadn't returned from his meeting with his client, and Leo told her he'd be home after dinner. As Leo drove them away from the ranch, the house faded and a small pang of nervousness gripped Merrie. She was all for getting clothes but hadn't prepared for the anxiety of leaving the safe confines behind.

"You all right?" Leo asked.

"Not really."

"You want me to turn back?"

She shook her head. "It's ridiculous. Right? Letting this linger in my mind."

"It's normal, Merrie. Have you ever heard of the Nimerigar?"

She shook her head.

"They are a Shoshone legend, small magical creatures who are aggressive in nature, shooting poisoned arrows into people. The literal translation is people eaters."

"And this is comforting how?"

He smiled. "It is easy to imagine this Axe person as a Nimerigar...an annoying little creature wreaking havoc with your sense of security."

"And how does one kill a Nimerigar?"

"Just hit them on the head. They're tiny, after all."

His words brought a sense of lightness, easing her mind. She settled back in her seat, looking forward to the shopping trip. He drove to Wal-Mart, simply because that was really the best place to buy everything she needed. She started with clothes, grabbing two pairs of jeans and several shirts, then socks, panties and bras. Leo lingered at the sexier lingerie and she rolled her eyes. Next, she made sure to grab a sweater and jacket, since nights were often chilly. She picked out a pair of sensible sneakers before heading over to the personal hygiene area. She needed a toothbrush, a hairbrush, deodorant and of course, concealer for the faint bruise still lingering on her cheek. Everything else, like soap and toothpaste, she could use whatever the guys had available. The total would be enough that she was going to work her ass off to repay them. However, between helping Leo in the office and doing their housework, she'd already figured it all out and hoped to pay back their kindness.

She pushed the cart to the checkout lane and eyed the items she'd picked out, going through the mental list again.

"I could put back two shirts—"

"Don't you dare," Leo warned. "You barely have anything."

"I have more than enough," she assured him. "And I will work hard to pay you back."

"Stop," he ordered.

"I don't like to feel beholden."

He frowned. "Do you think Braden and I are doing this to make you feel *beholden*?"

"You're good people."

He snorted. "That wasn't an answer."

"Of course not," she admitted.

The woman in front of them finished her sale and left. The cashier began ringing up Merrie's purchases. With every click of the scanner, Merrie winced and when the total came up, she almost fainted. Leo just smiled at the cashier and swiped his credit card through the holder. A second later, he signed the electric pad then he gathered the bags while her mouth still hung open.

"Come on, Merrie," he said. "Grab that last bag."

It was a small one holding her personal items, and she hurried to catch up with him. It wasn't until she stepped outside that she forgot something very important. She came to a stop and bit her lower lip.

"What's wrong?" Leo asked.

"I, ah, forgot to pick something up," she said. "Something important for, um, that time of the month."

He struggled to contain his grin. He turned and offered his ass to her.

"Grab my wallet and go back in to get them," he ordered. "I'll get the truck and wait for you here."

Merrie tried very hard not to think about the very firm ass cheek that she was touching as she pulled his wallet out. She turned away before he could see the blush on her cheeks and hurried back into the store.

Several minutes later, as she was leaving with her new purchase, she heard the sound of motorcycles and stopped dead in her tracks. Her heart sped up until she thought it would burst through her chest. She dropped her bag and spun around, trying to find the source of the sound. The bikes all pulled up at the intersection stoplight, the riders clearly visible. Panic exploded within her and she scrambled toward the protection of the Wal-Mart, knowing *he* couldn't take her with so many witnesses around. Intent on avoiding the bikers, she ran into a tall man and sprawled backward on the sidewalk.

"Are you okay, ma'am?" a deep voice rumbled.

Merrie blinked and stared up at the man, her eyes widening in shock at the cop. A badge hung clipped on his belt and a gun rode the holster on his hip. His caring green eyes crinkled at the corners as he held out his hand to help her up. Fear spiraled through her and she couldn't do a single thing to help herself escape.

"Ma'am?" the cop asked softly.

He crouched and she scrambled to her feet.

"Are you all right?"

She nodded frantically.

"Merrie?" Leo called.

At his voice, relief flooded her. She groped for the bag she'd dropped then jumped into the passenger seat of Leo's truck. Leo waved at the cop and then drove off. "What's wrong?"

"M-motorcycles."

"I saw them," he replied. "Don't worry. They weren't the Demon Devils."

"How can you tell?"

"The way they were dressed."

That didn't make a lick of sense to her but she really didn't care. All that mattered was the fact that the bikers were going one way and she was heading in the complete opposite direction.

They drove for a while but she couldn't stop shaking. She sensed Leo's concerned glances and finally he pulled over onto the shoulder of the road. He drew her into his arms, holding her tightly, and the dam on her emotions finally broke. She cried out her fear, cried out the terror that had never left. She'd bottled it all inside, thinking she was over it and what she'd been through, but she'd only been fooling herself.

She'd almost *died*! There was still a possibility that Axe would find her, hurt her and finish the job he'd started. How could she resume her life with that hanging over her head? No matter how far she ran, it would always be in the back of her mind, and she'd be constantly looking over her shoulder.

Leo rocked her, pressing his lips in soothing kisses along her hairline. After a while, her sobs quieted then eventually died, leaving her feeling emotionally drained. She just wanted to lie down, close her eyes and sleep until tomorrow.

"Are you all right?" Leo asked softly.

"No. Yes." She sighed. "I guess for now I'm all right. Thank you."

He tightened his arms around her. "I'm here if you need me, even if it's just for a shoulder."

"It feels nice," she admitted, pulling back to look up at him. "I've never had someone let me borrow their shoulder. I've only ever had myself."

"Merrie," he whispered. "You don't have to be alone anymore."

She bit her bottom lip. "What does that mean, Leo? Because I'm starting to feel...something...for you and Braden. And that's... Shit, that's so wrong. Isn't it? I mean, you rescued me. You've been so nice. How do I know it's not just...? I don't know...gratitude?"

"I guess we just take things day by day," Leo replied. "May I ask something of you, Merrie?"

"What?"

"May I kiss you?"

Excitement zipped down her spine and butterflies erupted in her stomach. She gave a nod and watched as Leo bent his head toward her. At the last second, she closed her eyes and his lips settled on hers.

Leo moved his lips gently over hers, soft and incredibly hot. He traced her bottom lip with his tongue and she opened her mouth on a surprised sigh. He immediately deepened the kiss, sweeping his tongue in to dance with hers. For several long moments, he kissed her over and over, each time possessing her further and longer. At first, she was content to let him take the lead, but after a while, she grew bolder, twining her arms around his neck and pressing herself closer to him. She loved how he bent her back until she was almost lying on the truck bench, dominating and passionate.

When he finally ended the kiss and straightened, she stared at him through half-lowered lids.

"Wow," she murmured. "You're a great kisser, Leo."

"Yeah? Maybe it's because I had a wonderful partner."

She took a deep breath and settled into his side. He tightened his arm around her as he drove the rest of the way to the ranch.

Chapter Eight

The next morning dawned bright and early, and Merrie had a hard time not bouncing around in her excitement to start work. Leo had left before dawn on an emergency call but he was expected back soon to show her around the office. As she was in the kitchen brewing coffee, a knock sounded at the door. Braden told her to stay out of sight and opened the door.

"Hello," the man said. "I'm Detective Clark Christianson from Cheyenne. I'm looking for Mr. Braden McClintock."

"That's me," Braden answered.

"Hello, Mr. McClintock. I work in organized crimes and my captain brought your report of a biker gang related attack to my attention. May I come in so we can talk?"

"Of course," Braden said.

Merrie moved into the kitchen archway to look at the man. He didn't look like a cop. He certainly didn't look like a cop who could handle the biker, Axe, either. He was of average height and build, balding. Bags drooped under his eyes, giving him a tired look, and the brackets by his mouth hinted that he clenched his teeth a lot.

"It's okay, Merrie," Leo gestured for her to come and sit next to him. "He's from Cheyenne."

While she and Braden settled on the couch, Detective Christianson sat on the recliner. He pulled out a notebook and pen.

"Why don't you start from the beginning?" the detective offered.

Braden took her hand in his and gave her an encouraging nod. She took a deep breath.

"I was lost and didn't have a signal on my cell phone," she said. "I saw a bar and figured I'd call the police for help, so I circled around back where I found a payphone. When I got out of my car, two men were talking and shaking hands. Then…the man with the goatee, whom the other man called Axe, attacked me. He…hit me. When I told them I was lost and was only going to call the police for help, the other man — the one with a long gray beard — said Axe had to clean up his mess and make sure no one found my body."

Braden tightened his fingers around hers. When she glanced at him, fury blanketed his face. She used her thumb to sooth the back of his hand.

"Please, go on," Detective Christianson murmured.

"He punched me and I blacked out. Sometime later, I came to and realized I was in the back of my car, heading somewhere. I got out of my bindings, jumped from the car, and I ran into the woods."

The detective arched both eyebrows.

"I found her on the dirt road south of here, the one separating my land from the Hamilton's," Braden said.

"Are you usually out on that road?"

"Sometimes. The Hamilton's buy horses from me."

"Did you go to the hospital, Miss Walden?"

She shook her head. "The man—Axe—said the cops were in his pocket. I didn't want to chance going to the hospital in case the police were looking for me."

"So no one knows you're here? Who put the cast on your wrist?"

"My brother," Braden answered. "He's a veterinarian. Hold on. We took photos."

He got up and headed toward his office then came back out a moment later with his digital camera. He turned it on and brought up the pictures of Merrie. He handed it over for Detective Christianson to look at them.

The detective scrolled through each frame slowly. Occasionally he'd flick his gaze to her as if he were comparing the photo from then to how she looked now. His mouth flattened in to a grim line. When he was done, he turned off the camera and sat it on the coffee table.

"Is it possible to have those pictures?"

"I can email you a copy," Braden offered.

The detective nodded. "I'd appreciate that. Was Axe driving your car?"

"No. It was some other man. I didn't get a look at his face but he had a snake tattoo on his right forearm." She drew in a shaky breath.

Braden slipped his arm around her and she relaxed into his warmth.

"Snake tattoo?" Christianson looked at the two men. "Have you seen a man with a tattoo like that?"

Braden shook his head. "We don't really associate with that crowd."

Christianson nodded. "It was a brave thing you did, Miss Walden, jumping out of that car."

"If I'd stayed in it, I'd be in an unmarked grave right now. Braden and his brother Leo rescued me."

He leaned forward and looked her straight in the eye. "The way I see it, you rescued yourself. Do you have any clue why they targeted you?"

She shook her head. "None. Although Braden and Leo think it might be some type of initiation to get into their club."

"The club on Route 18, right? The Demon Devils?"

"Yes," Braden confirmed.

"I know the club well. They've been on our radar for some time. Unfortunately, they're very good at evading the law." Detective Christianson stood. He pulled out two cards and handed one to her and the other to Braden. "I'll start my own investigation into this Axe character, as well as the local police. Just stay here out of sight and don't talk to anyone until I say otherwise. Understood?"

Braden stood as well and held out his hand. The two men shook firmly then Braden escorted him out of the door.

* * * *

When Clark Christianson slid behind the wheel of his rental car, he pulled out his cell phone and dialed the number to his brother's burner phone.

"Did you find her?" Axe asked, forgoing a greeting.

"Yes. You did a fucking number on her, you shit."

"Obviously not enough. She's still alive."

"They have pictures and there's more than enough to arrest your sorry ass."

"You're not going to arrest me. Otherwise, I'll be singing how you've always looked the other way when it comes to your baby brother. Now, where is she?"

"Like I'm going to fucking tell you. I'm still a cop, Axe."

"Don't screw around, Clark!" Axe yelled over the line. "Tell me where the girl is so I can get back to business."

"And what business is that, Axe? Unlike the clueless girl I just interviewed, I happen to know why your panties are in a twist. I work in organized crimes, remember? And outlaw motorcycles clubs fall under that jurisdiction. What's the angle?"

"None of your business. And if the cops come snooping around or if I get fucking arrested for this petty shit, then I'm not the only one going down in flames. Got it, brother?"

Clark clicked off the call and tossed the phone onto the passenger seat. Two weeks. Two fucking weeks and he got saddled with his brother's fucking mess. He started up the car and wondered how he could string this along until his retirement day arrived. Then he could write this off as a bogus investigation and go fishing.

Chapter Nine

When Leo got home about twenty minutes later, he and Braden sat to talk about Detective Christianson while Merrie made breakfast. It might be sexist, but she liked the feeling of taking care of the two men, cooking their breakfasts while they talked at the table. Her broken wrist wasn't as much of a hindrance as she'd thought it would be. She still had use of her fingers. She served their plates piled with eggs, bacon and toast, and set cups of piping hot coffee and glasses of orange juice next to them. Braden sat at the head of the table, Leo to his right and she took the seat on Leo's left.

For a moment, she just watched both men eat. She couldn't help the feeling of contentment that came over her, as if she had found the place where she belonged. All of her life she'd been looking out for only herself but deep down she'd always wanted a home and loved ones — family.

The rush of emotions the thought evoked gave her a sense of vulnerability and she bowed her head to eat. Her left hand was becoming stronger the more she

sucked. She gave them a sunny smile, pushing her dismay down deep.

"I like working," she said. "I like keeping busy. Come on, Leo. I want to help you out."

Then she swept past them, across the porch and down the steps, heading over to Leo's truck to wait for him. Braden came out onto the porch and watched them leave.

* * * *

"I don't really set appointments," Leo said as he turned off the alarm to the office and flipped on the light. "The only time I do is for vaccines and various shots and that's because I don't want owners to become lazy and forget. Most of the time people just bring their pets by. All my on-call appointments are usually for herd animals."

Merrie looked around the waiting room. A wall divided two sections, one for cats and the other for any other animals. The décor was simple and easy to maintain, which was probably crucial for any accidental animal messes.

"Interesting way you've divided the sitting room," she said.

"Many cats spook easily, especially when they're in a carrier," he explained. "Giving them a little privacy from leashed dogs seemed like the right thing to do."

The reception area was behind a low counter. It held a phone, a computer, a copier and a fax and nothing else. Very Spartan but very efficient.

"No files?"

He shook his head. "I went paperless. I work with a tablet then back up my data every night to the server. The server is then backed up with another company."

"Very eco-friendly," she said.

"Yes, and the way of the future. You don't have to learn any of that. Mainly what you'll do is answer phones and make appointments in my calendar for pets needing various shots. Oh, which reminds me, let me take out those stitches later. I don't want to leave you with railroad marks."

"Okay," she said. "They're starting to itch anyway."

Leo showed her how to lead the patient to an exam room then how to send him a message on his tablet about who his next patient would be and their location. Just before he left the reception, he pointed to the computer. "It can get boring here so you can browse the Internet. I don't mind."

"Thanks," she said.

She didn't have time, however, to play much on the Internet because the first patient came in, a woman carrying a very fat Chihuahua. At ease greeting the woman, Merrie led her back to an exam room. She typed a quick email to Leo just as the door opened again.

It stayed fairly busy throughout the morning. She didn't know how Leo had managed without his assistant, a woman by the name of Patty, who was off celebrating her one-year anniversary. There were several pictures of her and her husband on their wedding day sitting around the computer, making Merrie a little envious of the happiness on Patty's face.

Merrie took several messages, mainly people wanting Leo to stop by when he had a chance to look over a sick cow, horse or goat. She made a few appointments. And although she was new to the veterinary world, she immediately fell in love with it.

* * * *

Over the next couple of days, she, Braden and Leo fell into a comfortable pattern. She'd cook breakfast every morning, head to the office with Leo, have lunch with him and Braden, then cook dinner at night. The men would clean up and afterward, they would watch the news before heading to bed. Sometimes Leo was called away for an emergency and sometimes Braden came home late from the barns, but Merrie had never felt more at peace in her entire life.

The only disturbance in her happy little world was the fact that the specter of Axe hung in the back of her head. Her one and only trip to the outside world had terrified her and she hoped the men never asked her to leave.

Each night she dreamed of them. The dreams were always filled with erotic images and desires. Sometimes she was sandwiched between them, both men filling her at the same time, loving her until she was breathless with desire. Sometimes it was one then the other. She'd wake up with an ache between her thighs that wasn't satisfied by quick masturbation sessions.

While her pulse raced with excitement, she brought her hand up to her mouth, caressing her lips, slowly sliding a finger inside the moist warmth to suck on it, getting it nice and wet. She pretended it was Braden's finger or Leo's, teasing her. Taunting her.

She pulled her finger from her mouth to trail down her neck, her chest. The air hit the wet trail, cooling her skin. She reached the apex of her thighs and burrowed into the curls surrounding her sex. Moisture slicked her pussy lips, liquid proof that she wouldn't be able to last long. Merrie let her thighs fall open, pressed a finger inside, and her thumb against her clit.

Already her pulse quickened at the onslaught of the pleasure streaming through her body.

Her nipples hardened, pebbling into aching points that demanded attention. With one hand buried between her thighs, she cupped her breast with the other. She thought about Braden and Leo, imagined one sucking on her tits while the other buried his face in her pussy. It should be wrong to fantasize about two men, but it just felt so right. Pleasure spiraled through her body. She bucked her hips at the image of both men possessing her, fucking her. A breathless little moan escaped as she slipped another finger into her pussy and applied pressure against her clit.

She pinched her nipple, tugging on the sensitive nub. The bite of pain only added the eroticism and she wanted more than anything to be filled with cock, but since that was denied, she sped up her thumb's frantic clit rubbing until she bucked her hips harder in a desperate attempt to come.

The pressure built up and up, boiling over, until she came with a shout. Her climaxes always felt great, but empty. Her body knew the difference between masturbation and actual loving and she'd fall asleep to dreams of both men surrounding her.

Chapter Ten

Sheriff Givon Halloran pulled his truck up along the side of the squad car belonging to one of his deputies and shut the engine off. The office had received a phone call from a hiker who had reported a burned-up car shell located along some high boulders near the trail.

He walked around where he could stare down the hill. Needing a better look, he carefully maneuvered down the gravel path into the shade of the tall maple and ash trees then around to the boulders where yellow crime scene tape roped off the area. Behind it, a car still smoldered.

His deputy snapped photos of the charred husk, latex gloves already on his hands. The kid was fresh out of the academy but he was a hard worker and seemed to be a stickler for protocol.

"What do we have, Jack?" Givon asked.

"The license plate is gone, probably taken off to hinder identification. But the good news is the VIN number hasn't melted, so we can trace the car," Jack told him. "Unfortunately, everything else is ash."

"At least there isn't a body." Givon walked around the car then turned to where the ass end pointed toward the road. "So the car was pushed off the road then set on fire. What evidence do you think the person was trying to conceal?"

Jack shrugged. "At least the person stayed around to make sure the whole forest didn't catch on fire."

"There is that."

Givon leaned over what used to be the windshield. He asked to borrow Jack's notebook and pen then proceeded to write down the vehicle identification number. He tore out the paper and handed it and the pen back.

"I'm going to run this," he said, holding up the paper. "Will you handle cleaning this up?"

"Sure," Jack said.

Givon decided to walk up the hill, following the path the car must have taken to see if there were any clues, but he didn't spot anything. In his truck, he booted up his dashboard computer and typed in the VIN. A name and face immediately popped up from the motor vehicle database and he stared at it in shock.

Merrie Christmas Walden.

It wasn't so much that her name was funny as it was the fact he'd seen the same girl on the screen the other day coming out of Wal-Mart. The look of terror on her face had stayed with him for some time. He'd thought about calling Leo Cloud Dancer to see if she was okay, but decided not to freak her out any more than she already seemed to be. Now, it looked like he'd have to make a trip over to Leo's and Braden's place after all.

He stepped out of his truck and called down to Jack. "Hey, I know the owner. I'm going to go interview her."

"Who is she?"

"A woman by the name of Merrie Walden."

"And she's around here? Want me to go?"

Givon shook his head. "I'll see you later."

He got back in his truck and rumbled off.

* * * *

About half an hour later, he pulled up in front of Braden's and Leo's farmhouse. The house was old, having been in the McClintock family for several generations. It held a type of old world charm, painted crisp white with black shutters. A large willow tree helped shade the two stories. He walked up the porch steps to the front door and knocked.

Leo opened it and gave him a perplexed look. "Hello, Sheriff. What can I do for you?"

"Hi, Leo. The other day at Wal-Mart, you called out to a woman who bumped into me," he said easily. "Merrie Walden. Do you know where she is?"

Leo shuffled his feet and Givon's senses sharpened. Braden appeared behind him.

"What do you want with Merrie?" Braden asked.

The hackles rose on the back of his neck. He rested his hand on the butt of his gun.

"Her car was found about half an hour from here off a hiker's trail," Givon said, moving his gaze back and forth between both men. "I'd like to ask her some questions."

"If we see her again, I'll be sure to pass along the information," Braden answered.

Givon's bullshit meter went haywire. He narrowed his eyes. "Is she in trouble?"

"Why would you ask that?"

"Look, her car was torched, she had a cast on her wrist, and she was terrified of me."

The two men gave each other a measured look. Annoyance sluiced through him and he put his hands on his hips.

"Is she here?" he demanded.

"Listen, Givon—"

"Oh, now it's Givon? Come on, guys. We've known each other our whole lives. What the hell is going on?"

Braden reached into his pocket and pulled out a card. He handed it to Givon. Givon frowned as he read the name.

"If you have any questions, talk to that detective," Braden said.

"Cheyenne PD? Braden—"

Braden shook his head. "I can't talk about it, Givon. Just give that man a call. Okay?"

He shut the door, leaving him frustrated and staring at a little rectangular card. A lot of *what the fucks?* rolled through his head.

Chapter Eleven

"Braden, you have to give me some money," Merrie said frantically when Givon's police SUV disappeared down the road. "I don't know when I'll be able to pay you back but I will. Someday. I'll go to Florida. Is there a bus stop in Destiny? Can you take me? Shit! My purse. I don't even have a driver's license."

"Merrie—"

"Please, Braden!" She ran over to him and put her hands on his chest. She couldn't help begging. She began to pant a little in fear, which had the world spinning. "That cop knows. Axe has found me."

"Shh, Merrie," Braden murmured, pulling her into the circle of his arms. "That was just Givon Halloran, the sheriff of Destiny. I highly doubt he's on the take."

"Someone is!" she cried. "*He* told me that."

"And he's not going to find you," Braden comforted her, his voice hard and determined. "I'd give you anything, everything, if I thought it was the best decision. But Givon mentioned they found your car and I'm sorry, but it was burned."

Her chin quivered and tears welled up in her eyes.

"I've lost everything," she whispered. "My purse, my money, my possessions… It's all gone."

"Shh," he soothed again. "It's going to be okay."

"It's *not* okay! He's going to find me and he's going to hurt me again. I need to get as far away from Wyoming as possible because he'll hurt you too. Oh, I was so stupid to stay here for this long. I've got to go—"

Braden shut her up by kissing her. One minute she was raving like a lunatic and the next moment he claimed her mouth with his. At first, she didn't respond as surprise rippled through her. She simply took in the fact that her stoic, taciturn cowboy was, in fact, kissing her. She wrapped her arms around his neck and opened her mouth, letting her tongue meet the seam of his lips. He opened immediately and swirled their tongues together. It was different from Leo's kiss but no less sensual. Her fear melted into desire and, when he pulled back to stare at her with his blazing blue orbs, her fear evaporated.

He swept his gaze over her head and she suddenly remembered Leo.

Crap.

She withdrew her arms and Braden's fell away. She took a deep breath and turned. Leo watched them with his head tilted to one side, as if he were observing something fascinating.

"Leo, I'm sorry."

"About what?" he asked.

She took a deep breath. "I'm not playing one brother against the other. I swear it. The kiss… It just happened."

"What is she talking about, Leo?" Braden asked.

"I've often wondered why Tam Apo led you to our door," Leo said, a soft smile playing at the corner of his mouth. "The Great Father often leads destiny to us but seldom reveals why. I've seen the way you look at Braden and him at you when he thought no one was looking. I know how you feel in my arms. It's been confusing and troublesome but I think I understand now."

"Well, that's great," Braden said. "Perhaps you wouldn't mind sharing. I'm a little confused."

"The earth, the sun and the moon exist in harmony," Leo explained. "It is a perfect trinity for life—and for love."

"Come on," Braden scoffed. "Do you truly believe that a threesome equals love?"

Leo raised an eyebrow. "I think you shouldn't be so cynical."

"I don't know, Leo," Braden muttered. "I don't know if I'm ready for that."

Leo shrugged. "We should try. Shouldn't we?"

"Hello, standing right here," Merrie said a bit angrily. "It's annoying when you two are talking about something that involves me but I have no clue what's going on."

"Don't you?" Leo asked her softly. "You admitted to me you have feelings for the both of us."

She shook her head. "That makes me messed up. Doesn't it?"

"I don't think so," Leo said. He looked at his brother. "Braden?"

"He's talking about something deeper growing between us," Braden said. "I'm a little hesitant, though. How old are you, Merrie?"

She blinked. "I'm twenty-three."

"Don't, Braden," Leo warned. "She's nothing like Samantha."

"Who's Samantha?" Merrie asked.

"She's my ex-wife," Braden replied. "We gotten married way too young and after a while, she couldn't handle life on the ranch. She didn't like the isolation. She expected me to get out, explore the world. In the end...I couldn't hold onto her."

Merrie's heart ached for him. "I'm sorry, Braden. But it's true. I do feel something for you and Leo."

"You'll change your mind."

He'd stated it so matter-of-factly that it hurt her.

"If this progresses," he added, "then one day you'll decide you can't live here anymore—that you don't want to settle down so young." He shook his head. "I can't go through that again."

"Pardon me, but you don't know anything about what I want. I won't lie and say that in the beginning, when I first woke up, being safe was my number one priority. Of course it was—I'd just escaped certain death. And I was also concerned that my attraction was based on you and Leo saving me. But I'm past the desperate gratitude, Braden. What I feel isn't that."

"Well, it certainly isn't what Leo's proposing."

"Why do we have to define more than it is right now?" She cocked her head. "I think the bigger question is, why me?"

"What do you mean?"

She shrugged. "I'm nobody. A person you saved on the road. What makes me special in your eyes?"

He stayed silent for a long moment. "You're brave," he finally said.

Merrie took his hands in hers. "Braden, I'm not Samantha. I may not have been here long, but I already know I never want to leave. I feel the love and the warmth of this ranch, of the childhood you and Leo must have had, and it's beautiful."

She could see he wanted to believe her. But there was a world of hurt in his eyes that she didn't know how to banish. Hopefully, time would help whittle away his insecurities.

He cupped her face. "You're so young."

"Not so young I haven't lived," she replied. "Not so young that I don't know what I want."

"Would you like to try to make this work between us?" he asked.

Once again, she looked between both men and read the sincerity in their gazes. Happiness swelled inside her as well as uncertainty. She'd never considered a ménage relationship and had no idea how to navigate the waters.

"Have you ever done this before?" she asked.

"No," Leo said. "But learning is half the fun."

Braden swung her up into his arms and she squealed with delight. She wrapped her arms around his neck. He marched up the stairs with Leo following. At the top, he hesitated and glanced at his brother.

"Mine," Leo said. "I've got a king-size bed."

Braden turned left and marched into Leo's room. She'd been in there once before when she'd grabbed some sweats and still marveled how different his room was compared to Braden's. Leo liked forest colors. Dark greens, browns and sunset red all blended beautifully together.

Braden placed her on the bed and began undressing her. He traced his hands over her curves, over her aching breasts, to her jeans. His long fingers brushed the skin under her fly, which sent off a thousand butterflies in her belly. He unbuttoned and unzipped her pants.

"Lift your hips, sweetheart," he murmured.

She obeyed and he shimmed the jeans over her hips, leaving her only in her bra and panties. Leo gently rolled her onto her side so he could unhook her bra and she pulled it off. Both men were careful not to bump into the bruises that still dotted her skin. Then Braden hooked his fingers in her panties and pulled them down, letting her step out of them before running his hands up her smooth legs. At his touch, she thanked the stars above she'd shaved that morning. Leo glided his hands up from her ankles to her ass where he kneaded her butt cheeks. He placed small kisses at the base of her spine then proceeded upward. Her back had always been sensitive and she shivered as he caressed her skin.

Braden ran his fingers gently through her hair. She loved the feel of his fingers soothing her scalp. He tipped her head back to kiss her, possessing her lips in a series of teasing kisses, letting his tongue dance with hers only to retreat then press back inside, like a little game he played so all her senses tingled. All she wanted to do was kiss him forever.

The men undressed quickly, and she took the moment to admire their muscled physiques. Strong arms, toned stomachs. Leo didn't have chest hair but Braden had a fine taper leading to his very impressive dick that jutted out proudly.

Leo pressed himself against her back and ran one hand over the curve of her bottom, allowing his fingers to slide between her ass cheeks to touch her intimately. With his thumb, he circled her tight muscle ring then pressed in a little. The pressure made her squirm. Easing his touch, he slid his fingers forward until he found her slit. There, he rubbed in feathery strokes that soon heated Merrie's blood and urged her juices to run. Now slick, he pressed his fingers inward.

Bending one finger, he rubbed along the back wall of her pussy while he found her clit with his other hand. In and out, he used his fingers to heighten her pleasure while Braden continued kissing her.

Truly sandwiched between them, Merrie knew nothing had ever felt so good, so right. Braden broke the kiss to rain more over her cheek and down her neck. He took her breasts in his hands, cupping them and teasing the nipples by pinching them. The ache between her thighs climbed quickly. He bent, taking one nipple in his mouth, licking and sucking on it until she was all but thrashing between them.

"You're so beautiful," Leo murmured. "Braden, feel how beautiful she is."

Braden teasingly trailed his fingers down her stomach and slid the tips through her pubic curls. When he found her slit, he slipped his middle finger into her warmth.

"Oh, yes," Braden breathed. "So wet. So tight. And beautiful."

"Oh," she sighed, tingling pleasure radiating upward from her sensitive pussy.

As he kissed her, he began fucking her with his finger, sliding it in and out of her slowly. Soon, she needed more, needed him to go faster, or harder, even deeper. The almost lazy glide of his finger wasn't enough.

"More," she said.

"Let me get the condom from my wallet," he murmured.

Braden halted and she moaned in protest. She didn't mean for him to stop. But the tearing of a foil wrapper alerted her that he wasn't done with her. She opened her eyes to find him staring at her, hunger burning in his gaze.

"I want you to ride me and suck Leo off," Braden said. "Can you do that, sweetheart?"

"Oh, yes." She looked over at Leo, who stroked his long cock as he watched them with hooded eyes.

Braden lay down, his cock ready for her and she lowered herself onto him. His large dick filled her, stretching her almost uncomfortably. She had to give herself a moment to adjust. He gripped her waist, allowing her find her center, before guiding her movements. Merrie loved being on top. She loved being able to look down at Braden and watch the pleasure blossom over his face.

He gasped. "You feel incredible."

Leo groaned, grabbing her attention, and she turned her head. Seeing him masturbate turned her on, reminding her of when she used him in her own fantasies. She reached over and replaced his hand with hers.

"Scoot closer," she whispered.

Leo did as she asked. He wasn't circumcised so she held back his foreskin and brought him into her mouth. She laved the tip, kissed the hole then used her teeth gently around the crown. Finally, she slurped him down. She'd never particularly loved giving head but Leo tasted especially good—dark, salty and all male.

"You do that too good, sweetheart," he said. "What about her pretty little cunt, Braden? Is she nice and tight?"

"Oh, God, yes," Braden gasped.

The dirty words really turned her on. It seemed to do the same to Braden, who held her waist as he hammered into her from beneath.

She gently stroked Leo's rock-hard erection, rising straight out from its nest of dark pubic hair. He pumped his hips, driving his cock into her hand. She gripped tighter, stroked harder. White fluid leaked from the tip and she eagerly lapped it up. The salty, bitter flavor burst across her tongue. Once more, she swallowed him down, taking as much as his big cock into her mouth as she could.

Their thrusts synchronized. Leo fucked her mouth and Braden guided her on his cock. She'd simply become the vessel for their sexual gratification— getting her own enjoyment in the process. Everything tightened. Her breathing came out in shallow pants. Her climax burst upon her, a wave of pleasure so intense all her muscles seized.

"Holy shit!" Braden gasped. "You're squeezing me so tight. I'm going to come."

His orgasm hit and he paused within her. He shook as he pulled her hips down while he surged up, thrusting as deeply as possible in her as he came and came.

Leo buried his fingers in her hair, taking control. She relaxed her throat muscles as much as possible as he chased his own ending. His rhythm faltered as he swelled in her mouth. At the last second, he pulled away as cum erupted from his cock to paint thick ropes on her chest.

As Leo collapsed beside her, Braden used the opportunity to leave her body and dispose of the condom. She snuggled into both of them, feeling replete.

Chapter Twelve

Braden turned on the oven light to give him enough illumination to make coffee. He should be bone-tired but he was too distracted to rest. His mind raced with what had just happened upstairs and it left him a little unsettled because he'd come to realize the heat of passion was one thing and reality was something quite different.

When the coffee had brewed, he poured a little milk in it then sat at the table letting his mind wander. What was he supposed to do or say now? Was he to believe that the Great Father, Tam Apo, had some great design that had led Merrie into his path? He'd never been a spiritual man but he didn't discredit Leo's beliefs. Hell, all one had to do was take a look at nature's beauty and wonder what had created such perfection. But he'd long ago given up in the faith that love conquered all. He didn't doubt love between a man and woman existed — his own parents were proof of that — but his parents had come from a different era and life in Destiny could be remote.

Not to mention the fact that Leo was involved in the mix. How the hell could he think a ménage relationship would work? Relationships took a great deal of effort, and having three people made the attempt triply difficult.

Merrie talked a good talk, but she was young. She had her whole life in front of her with different horizons to meet and mountains to climb. And he knew best, what happened when wanderlust settled into the soul. It made a person pack up in the middle of the night and drive away, never to return.

"Can't sleep?" Leo asked from the kitchen doorway.

Braden shook his head. Leo headed to the coffeemaker and poured himself a cup then sat across from Braden, studying him by the muted oven light. Leo studied him right back. Memories poured through Braden's head of when they'd been kids, when Leo would come with his father and the two boys would ride over the plains for hours. They'd talked about all sorts of things and shared confidences. When his family had all but adopted Leo, he'd become more than just a friend to Braden. They were brothers, regardless of blood.

"You're regretting what happened," Leo stated, as he blew on his coffee. He took a tentative sip of the hot brew.

"Aren't you?"

"No," Leo answered, a grin teasing the corners of his mouth. "I will admit I never thought I'd be sharing sex in the same bed with you, but your masculinity is safe with me."

"Good to know," Braden replied dryly.

"Come on, man. Don't be like this."

"Be like what?"

"Don't turn off your feelings," Leo answered. "You do it all the damn time. It's like you can't handle — or don't want to deal with — your emotions. What happened with Merrie is a good thing. She cares for both of us."

"She's grateful. That's all she is. And I should've been more responsible."

Leo raised one eyebrow. "Responsible? She's a grown woman."

"She's seventeen years younger than me. That's a helluva age difference, Leo."

"She's not Samantha."

"How do you know?" Braden demanded. "How do you know that once this mess is cleared up, she's not going to get the itch for something bigger? You're only deluding yourself if you think she's not attracted to us out of gratitude."

Leo compressed his mouth into a hard line. "All right. I'll bite. Let's say you're right and she decides living on this ranch isn't what she wants. Are you going to be relieved that you were right or are you still going to miss her? Because I don't think you can stop your heart from falling in love."

"Love?" Braden scoffed. "What did you plan on? Us living together in a three-way relationship forever?"

"I didn't have sex with her thinking it was just sex," Leo stated. "Did you?"

Braden pushed his coffee away and stood. "I'm stepping back, Leo. You and Merrie, that's how it ought to be, at least until she's out of danger. And I won't say 'I told you so' when she leaves."

Leo swore under his breath. "We went into that bedroom as three people. You'll hurt her by rejecting her."

"What happened tonight was a mistake."

"You can't possibly believe that! Braden—"

Braden held up a hand, halting Leo's speech. "This is for the best, Leo. I let my dick do my thinking earlier but you'll see I'm right and so will Merrie."

He left and headed back upstairs, even though he didn't feel like sleeping. He paused at the top and looked at Leo's closed bedroom door. His stomach seized with want and desire. Despite his words, all he wanted to do was crawl back into bed next to Merrie and spoon with her, kiss her awake and make love to her again. His cock grew so hard with arousal that he was sure he could hammer nails with it. But he didn't—he *couldn't*—go through heartache again.

Best to end it now.

He walked into his bedroom and shut the door.

* * * *

Merrie had never been so comfortable, so relaxed, in all her life. She blinked her eyes open and stretched. Alone in Leo's bed, she reached out to the warmth in the sheet, but the lack of heat indicated Braden had risen a while ago. She sat up, holding the sheet to her breasts, just as the door opened and Leo walked in.

She smiled, all warm and gooey inside. "I was lonely," she said.

He held out a cup of coffee. "Good morning, beautiful."

Pleasure rushed through her body at his words. She took the coffee and sipped it, loving how the heat and caffeine hit her system. "What time is it?"

He sat at the foot of the bed and studied her. "Six. I got a call from the Johnson farm. One of their cows somehow ended up tangled in barbed wire again so I have to head over there. Want to come with me?"

"Yes," she said. "Poor thing."

"Mmm," he murmured. "This is the third time. I keep telling Chuck that he doesn't need the damn barbed wire for cows, but the idiot doesn't listen to me."

She set her coffee mug on the nightstand then scooted forward and draped her arms around his neck. She studied his dark eyes.

"Are you okay?" she asked.

"Shouldn't I be asking you that question?"

"I'm okay," she said. "Although I'm a little surprised that I enjoyed it so much."

"Why?"

"Because I never thought of myself as anything other than a one man sort of woman. You know?"

Something dark passed over his face. Hesitation? Regret? Then he smiled brightly, leaving her to wonder if she imagined the slight reaction at all. "Society has placed a stigma on alternative lifestyles, but I see nothing wrong with a polyandrous relationship."

"Two stubborn men? Handling one can be a full-time job."

He bent his head and kissed her lightly on the lips. "Why don't you shower and get dressed?"

Merrie let her arms fall away from him as he stood. She got the distinct impression that he wanted to change the subject.

"I'll meet you downstairs."

"Leo? You *are* okay with what happened, aren't you?"

He nodded. "I guess I'm wondering what you see in me."

"Are you kidding? You're constant."

"I'm what?"

"Braden is...tough — strong. It's obvious that he takes no shit from anyone. You're the foundation, the glue that holds him together."

"I'm not sure how I feel being compared to glue."

She smiled. "I meant it in a good way."

"I know. There's just...things going on. I'll wait for you downstairs."

He left the bedroom, pulling the door behind him. She sat for a moment and listened to his boot steps receding down the stairs, the *thud, thud, thud* on the wooden floor suspiciously echoing the hollowness of the house. Where was Braden?

She got out of bed and gathered her scattered clothes. Not bothering to get dressed, she first went to her bedroom to clean up then headed into the bathroom. She stood in front of the mirror, staring at her reflection, trying to see if she looked any different after having a *ménage à trois*.

The bruise on her cheek had faded and the good nights of rest she'd been getting had helped erase the pinched, haunted look she'd had the previous week. The bruises around her torso had begun to fade as well. She looked kind of like a squash with ripe yellow skin.

Showering was still tricky with the cast. Merrie had to lay out what she needed and stand with her back to the shower, hanging her arm out of the curtain while only using one hand. By going slowly, she managed.

She dried and dressed but left her hair damp as she hurried downstairs, her sneakers not making any sound. Leo waited for her by the stove and handed over a plate containing a breakfast sandwich. Two slices of toast held an egg, bacon and a piece of cheese together.

"Thanks," she said. "I'm famished."

"After last night, I'm not surprised." He smirked.

She playfully smacked his arm. "It's entirely your fault. You and Braden wore me out."

That dark little frown briefly touched his face again. This time she couldn't shake the feeling that something was wrong, but Leo encouraged to her eat and, minutes later, she was buckling her seat beat as he put the truck into drive.

Unlike the last time when she'd left the ranch, she didn't have the urgent sense of desperation to go back and hide. Last night had given her a sense of belonging she'd never had before. Surely that monster, Axe, couldn't still hold out on his hope that he'd find and hurt her. Hopefully he'd realized that type of barbaric behavior wasn't tolerated by the law, because Merrie didn't want any other woman going through what she'd experienced.

The Johnson dairy farm wasn't that large, and since she'd worked on such a farm, this was familiar territory to Merrie. She saw the automated milk parlor as well as the refrigeration tanks that sat off to the side, ready to collect the milk pumped from the cows' udders. The cow stalls needed a good cleaning and she hoped that the owner, Chuck Johnson, would get to the task right away. Cows required fresh, dry, comfortable stalls. A man stepped out from the barn. His dirty overalls looked about a size too large, hanging off his rail-thin frame stuffed into rubber waders. His thinning hair, a non-descript color, lay plastered to his forehead from heat. He eyed her up and down before turning to Leo.

"She's out in the west pasture," Chuck said without a greeting.

Merrie read disdain in his face as he stared at Leo and her hackles rose. She knew immediately that Chuck Johnson didn't like Leo.

"All right," Leo replied softly. "Can we borrow your four-wheeler?"

"Sure," Chuck replied, thumbing to the side of the barn. "On the yonder side. Just follow the ridge line."

Leo nodded and walked where Chuck had indicated. Merrie followed.

"What's his problem?" she asked quietly.

"He doesn't like Indians."

Merrie blinked and stopped in her tracks, her mouth dropping slightly. "Are you serious? He's racist?"

"Many people are," he answered. "Those people take their pets all the way to Riverton to a non-Native vet. Chuck only deals with me because he doesn't have a way of transporting his cows."

"That's not right," she said. "It's the twenty-first century, for God's sake!"

"I don't do this for him," Leo stated. "I do it for that poor beast tangled up in metal that's cutting into her skin. Come on."

Dried mud splattered the ATV and it looked weather worn. Leo stowed his medical bag in the attached basket, straddled the machine, turned on the engine then waited as she got on behind him. He laid on the throttle with one hand. A moment later, wind blew her hair back as they raced over the land, headed toward the hurt cow.

Merrie didn't like the idea of anyone looking down on Leo. His people had more right to this land than assholes like Chuck Johnson did and she wished she could give the hateful little man a piece of her mind. But as soon as she saw the wounded animal lying on its side, she promptly forgot about everything but helping the poor creature.

She and Leo spent close to two hours untangling the wire from the cow's front hoof then bandaging it. Somehow, the cow had stepped through the opening of the fence line, but when she'd pulled it back, the wire had dug into the skin, crippling her.

"Poor baby." Merrie petted the animal on the forehead.

"I'll tell Chuck to bring her in, keep her in the barn for a few days. The bastard should've already untangled the poor beast instead of relying on me."

"Can we arrest him for animal cruelty?"

Leo shook his head grimly. "I've already measured the fence. The wire is strung properly at fifteen inches apart, which is the Wyoming livestock law. This cow was just unlucky."

He patted the cow's head soothingly before grabbing some antibacterial wipes to clean up.

"Ready to go?" he asked.

She gave the cow one last pat and stood. "Yes."

They drove back and parked the four-wheeler in its spot. While Leo went to talk with Chuck, Merrie walked toward the truck. She feared she'd say something bad to Chuck Johnson. Soon, Leo followed. He stored his medical bag in the bed then slid behind the wheel.

"That man is a jerk," he muttered, clearly frustrated. "He said he'll go check on the cow later but doesn't have a way to get her back to the barn. Damn fool. How does he not have a flatbed? Or a trailer?"

She rubbed his hand where he gripped the steering wheel. Leo had such a loving soul. He really cared about his animal patients and she loved that about him. They drove back to the office in silence. He unlocked the door and turned off the alarm before holding the door open for her.

"By the way," Leo said, digging in his pocket and producing a key. "I want you to have this."

"What is it?" she asked as she took it from him.

"The key to the office," he said. "Let me show you how to deactivate and set the alarm."

"Surely I don't need to know how to do that," she said. "Patty will be back in a few days."

Leo shook his head. "She called saying that she's pregnant and her OB wants her to stay home. She's older and it has been a difficult road for her to conceive, but I'm happy for her. She and Steve have been trying for a while, even before they got married."

"Oh. Then I'm very happy for her, as well."

Leo grinned. "It's okay, really. I have you now and I'm hoping this job is enough to convince you not to head to Cheyenne."

Something squeezed inside Merrie's chest and her heart pounded heavily with excitement. Dare she believe? "You want me to stay?"

He brushed a finger over her cheek. "Very much."

"Okay." Merrie nodded. She felt like she'd just won the lottery. "You sure Patty left voluntarily and you didn't fire her?"

"Honest to God," Leo said with a chuckle. "In fact, Patty was upset about abandoning me until I told her about you. Now, let me show you how the code works."

Merrie was a little hesitant to embrace how her dreams seemed to be coming true. She'd left her hometown to find a place to belong—a job she could care about and a place to call home. It seemed fantastical that one heinous act of violence was the catalyst to bringing it all together.

The rest of the day passed smoothly. It was vaccine day for many animals, which kept her hopping. She didn't have time to think about the previous night or the fact that she'd not seen Braden at all that day. She quickly learned how to draw up the vaccines for Leo and helped him with whatever she could. When the workday ended, Leo offered to take her to a restaurant for dinner. Feeling tired, she agreed and they ate at a diner north of Destiny, heading toward Riverton.

Their conversation remained light and Merrie made sure to avoid talking about what had happened the previous night. She didn't think it right to analyze it while missing one of the trio, and Braden was now very much a part of her life.

When they got back later that evening, eerie darkness engulfed the house. Crickets chirped, a soft breeze rustled the willow branches, and for a moment, Merrie thought it might be deserted.

"Braden must've gone to bed," Leo said, as he strode to the front porch.

Disappointed, she sighed, having missed Braden all day. Leo led the way up to his bedroom, where she hesitated, wondering if she was breaking some kind of unknown rule about sleeping with one man while the other was not around. Would there be private moments with Braden as well? So, she took Leo's hand and halted with him just as he closed the door, sealing them inside.

"This is all right, isn't it?"

He frowned, confused. "What do you mean?"

"Braden's not here."

Understanding dawned and he smiled at her. "Yes, it is all right, Merrie. Above everything, there's trust. All right?"

"All right. If that's the case, then stay just like that."

Amusement lit up his face but he did as she'd asked. Merrie began undressing him, kissing his skin wherever she exposed it. The shirt slid down his arms to land in a heap on the floor, followed by his belt. She kneeled to help him out of his pants and underwear and gasped as his cock sprang up, the tip already leaking fluid. She gave the head a quick lick, collecting the moisture before she pushed him back onto the bed. He gave a little groan. Merrie took off his shoes and socks to slide off the rest of his clothes.

"Scoot up the bed," she ordered.

He did so, fisting his dick and pushing the foreskin down to slowly massage his shaft. As he met her gaze, she enjoyed him pleasuring himself.

She performed a little strip-tease, even though there wasn't any music, but hunger lit up his face so any embarrassment she had drifted away. Finally naked, she crawled on her hands and knees over his body, taking another lick of his cock tip. He moaned and thrust his hips up, so she went down on him, swallowing his large cock as far as she could go. After a few minutes of making him moan, she released him and continued on her journey until she sat on his lap. His dick pressed along her ass cleft and the thought that she'd like to explore that area one day drifted through her mind, but then he kissed her and everything else faded from her head.

She sat astride his legs, her hair flowing loose around her face and shoulders. The position thrust her breasts out, toward his mouth, and he eagerly accepted the invitation. He sucked on each nipple until they stood raw and turgid from the delicious torment.

He collected her hair in one hand and yanked her head back, not causing pain but allowing him better access to slide up her torso with his tongue, taking nibbles along the way until his mouth met hers. Leo swept his tongue in to duel with hers as if he were trying to exert his dominance. Merrie was more than happy to surrender to such bliss.

He trailed his fingers over her hips then across her thighs to find the wetness oozing from her pussy. Merrie shuddered, and he delved his fingers deeper to find her G-spot. She rocked her hips as his hard cock slid into her crack while he teased her clit with his fingers.

His body all hard muscles over smooth skin, Leo maneuvered his jutting cock between her thighs. She reached behind her to grasp it, tracing the lines and contours, learning how it responded to her touch. She captured some of his pre-cum on a finger and brought it to her lips. She loved how he tasted.

He reached over to the nightstand and opened the drawer to pull out a condom. Next, he guided her to kneel forward so he could slip it over his cock. Then he lowered her over his shaft.

Excitement gripped her stomach as she sank on him, her pussy practically grabbing and pulling him inside her. He held her still for a moment to allow her to adjust to his girth, before he propelled her hips — back and forth, very tenderly and slowly.

Needing to move, she rolled her hips. Leo let out a moaning-hissing noise that she took as a good sign. She leaned over to gently bite his earlobe and that was all it took to break the slow and easy façade. He pumped her up and down on his cock — in and out, in and out — until Merrie wasn't sure if it was him out of control or her. All she did know was how incredible it felt to be with him. She gripped her inner walls around him so tightly a squelching sound occurred with each thrust.

"Ah, Leo," she breathed just as her climax hit. It coursed through her, bringing exquisite pleasure.

"Merrie!" He gasped just as he surged against her, shuddering his release.

After a moment, he relaxed and tucked her sweaty body against him. She could feel both their hearts beating frantically. He took off the used condom and tossed it in the wastebasket next to his bed.

"Will you sleep with me?"

"Of course," she answered drowsily. "I wish Braden was here too."

Leo didn't answer as she drifted off to sleep.

Chapter Thirteen

Braden left the house before dawn, wanting to get as far away from Merrie and Leo as possible. Damn if he hadn't been right about her being fickle, and even though he should have felt a small amount of vindication, hurt battered his heart. He'd had to listen to them last night and the memories of how Merrie had come apart in his arms, how tight her pussy had been around his dick, had crashed over him painfully.

To know that she'd gotten over him so quickly, that she'd turned her back so easily on him, cut him to the core and he tried to shake that off. He had no reason to feel such betrayal because he was the one who'd backed off. He was the one who'd given Leo the go-ahead.

He drove to the barn and parked, wishing it was as easy to turn off his thoughts. He planned to ride all day so he wouldn't bump into either of them. Braden greeted his ranch hand, who had just begun to clean the stalls. Usually he'd help, but today he couldn't. He needed to be out on the range, away from everyone.

He saddled his horse and mounted, then galloped off toward the eastern fields so he could check on the other horses. Crisp morning air filled his lungs and it helped settle his mind. How was he going to live with Merrie and Leo, who were now together? He felt sure he'd be able to bury his emotions deep but that didn't mean he wanted to be slapped upside the head each time he saw her — or saw them together.

Of course, it was just a matter of time before Merrie headed to Cheyenne, back to the life that she really wanted. Friends, parties, men her own age — how could she not want all that? She was only twenty-three with her whole life in front of her. Once she got bored of ranch life, she'd be gone.

Just like Samantha.

Through the day, he checked his horses, ate a power bar at lunch and enjoyed the solitude that only wide-open spaces could allow. And he almost forgot about what had driven him out here to begin with. When twilight began to fall, he reined in toward the barn. He dismounted about half a mile away and walked his mount to cool him down. He spent a couple more hours finding odd jobs to do — anything to keep him from going back to the house. Eventually his stomach protested too much so he got back in his truck and drove home. The dashboard read a little past nine o'clock and all he wanted to do was eat, shower and sleep.

Lights glowed in the kitchen and when he went inside, Merrie stood cleaning up the kitchen surfaces. Just seeing her hurt his heart and he was half tempted to starve himself just so he wouldn't have to face talking with her. What would she say? What would he say?

"Oh, hey!" she greeted, a warm smile not only gracing her lips but shining from her eyes.

"Hi," he greeted coolly. "Is there any food?"

Her smile slipped and she regarded him oddly. "Yes. Let me heat it up for you. Sit."

"Let me go wash my hands," he said. He used the downstairs bathroom, taking a little longer than necessary to clean up. When he walked back into the kitchen, a plate full of meatloaf, potatoes and vegetables waited for him. Merrie sat in the chair to his right, a cup of tea in her hands.

He wished she wasn't there. It was hard enough keeping his hands off her, let alone the temptation of her only a few inches from him. But when she smiled, he felt himself walking toward her like a moth drawn to a flame, helplessly caught in her heat.

He sat at the table and began to eat, doing his best to ignore her. Her fresh scent drifted over him and his dick stood at attention. Holy hell. How was he supposed to pretend she didn't affect him?

"I haven't seen you in almost two days," she said, lightly touching his hand. "I've missed you.

Braden frowned and moved his hand away. He took another bite to give himself time from what she'd said.

"Didn't Leo talk to you?" he asked after he'd swallowed.

"Talk to me about what?"

He sighed and rose, walking to the fridge to grab a beer. He twisted the lid off and downed half of it in one, long drink.

"You should eat more before you drink it all," Merrie warned. "Otherwise you're going to be tipsy."

"Damn it," Braden swore. "I never thought Leo was such a coward."

"What're you talking about? What's wrong, Braden?"

"Where's Leo?"

"He said he had some things to do at the office. Why? Hey, talk to me, Braden," she stressed.

"This," he said, gesturing between her and him. "Isn't going to work."

She flinched as if he'd struck her and it made him feel like a heel.

"I don't understand," she said, clearly confused.

"I told Leo I was stepping back," he said quietly.

"You...what? What does that mean?"

"It means we had a fantastic night together, but we need to be practical. Leo has this idea that we can all be together, that you're going to stay. And I know how impossible that is."

Her mouth dropped open and he read the surprise on her face. Slowly, she shook her head.

"What did I do wrong?"

"Nothing," he said. "I just know how this is going to end and I'd rather not get my heart broken again."

She blinked, her eyes huge in her pale face. "So this isn't about seeing if a three way relationship could work. It's about our age difference, isn't it? You still think I want to leave."

"Eventually, you will. Maybe not right now, but once this Axe person is caught, I'm pretty sure you'll be itching for the twenty-something lifestyle."

She surged to her feet and anger turned her cheeks red. "You condemn me for my age but out of the two of us, you're the one acting immature."

"Perhaps we should talk later—"

"Oh, no. You don't get to hide." Her face flared red. "We had something pretty incredible the other night and now you've decided I'm not good enough?"

"I never said you're not good enough!"

"This," she said, indicating the space between them, "tells me everything I need to know. You don't get to fuck me then decide a relationship is too messy, not even if it's a three-way relationship."

He turned away and set his beer down then leaned against the counter and hung his head. God, he was confused. He wanted to pull her into his arms and beg her forgiveness but his brain kept warring with his heart.

"Braden, please don't do this," she whispered.

He straightened. "I won't stand in your way with Leo. You both have my blessing, for as long as it lasts."

"May I ask you a question?"

"Of course," he said warily.

"When you were twenty-three, did you ever want to leave this ranch?"

He shook his head. "No, never."

"Then how can you doubt me when I feel as emphatically as you did then?"

He pursed his lips. "Well played, Merrie. But you're a woman. It's different."

"You're a coward," she spat. She didn't even wait for him to comment. Instead, she spun and stormed away. A few seconds later, the front door slammed. Part of him wanted to go after her and beg her to forgive him for his stupidity and another part of him wanted to punch something until he bled.

But he didn't do either of those things. He picked up his plate and dumped the rest of his dinner in the trash before washing everything. Then he headed up stairs and locked himself in his bedroom.

* * * *

Merrie sat on the porch swing and stared out at the night, unable to stop the tears flowing down her cheeks. Her emotions fluctuated from despair to anger. In fact, she was so mad she didn't know what to do except sit there and cry.

She understood about being scared and wary when it came to trusting someone. Hell, her own mother often forgot she had a daughter that she needed to feed. When her mom had ended up overdosing on heroine, Merrie had been sent to live with her Uncle Clarence but he'd died the following year, leaving her alone again. She'd dated a lot of guys, hoping one clicked with her so she wouldn't have to be alone anymore, only to realize they'd only wanted to screw her without any deeper feelings involved, thus earning her a bad reputation. Like mother, like daughter.

But she didn't understand how Braden could turn his back so easily when she knew they had a deep connection. She'd seen the pain on his face, the longing in his eyes when he'd looked at her. And to hear him dismiss what they shared had really cut her to the quick.

Leo's truck pulled into its spot and the lights flicked off. Leo stepped from the truck and sighed as he approached her.

"I take it he's still being an ass?"

Merrie wiped her cheeks. "Why didn't you tell me?"

"Because I was hoping he'd stop being an ass. He doesn't mean it, you know. He's just scared."

"Yeah? Well, newsflash—so am I. Having this type of relationship wasn't in my plans. I'm sure they weren't in yours either."

He sat next to her on the swing and rocked it gently. "What happened?"

"Basically he gave me to you, which by the way, thanks for asking. I'm not a door prize, you know."

"Give him a few days," Leo said.

"And then what? We live happily ever after? I can't do that if he's always going to think I'm going to leave. The only reason *to* leave would be because of him! Doesn't he get that?"

"I'm sorry, Merrie."

She stood. "There's nothing to be sorry about. In the beginning, I wanted to leave because I was petrified of Axe finding me. Then I stayed because I felt safe with you two. Now I have feelings for both of you and if one of you shuns me then I can't stay."

"Merrie—"

"If you don't mind," she snapped. "I'd rather be alone right now."

She left him there in the dark and headed up to her room. She didn't want one man over the other and she refused to put Leo in that kind of position. Damn Braden. It was just like a man to twist everything out of proportion.

Chapter Fourteen

Givon grabbed the phone and punched the line on hold. "Hello, this is Sheriff Halloran."

"Hello, Sheriff, I'm Captain Bruce Buckner with the Cheyenne PD."

"Thank you for returning my call. I've recently discovered the burned-out shell of a car and the VIN was traced back to a woman named Merrie Walden. I was informed through a third party that you have a detective in Destiny investigating and I'm slightly disturbed that I've yet to meet this detective."

"Clark hasn't checked in with you?"

"No, sir, he hasn't. I've called the number on his cell but I've not been able to touch base."

"My detective is working on the case," Captain Buckner assured him. "He's investigating you, so it's possible he's gathering evidence."

"Evidence? Need I remind you I am a sheriff of another county? Some common courtesy is demanded. Why don't you inform me what's going on, Captain?"

"We had a call come through about a woman allegedly assaulted by a biker. The woman was informed the Destiny police force was...ah...on the take and she shouldn't expect help. So I sent one of my detectives down to assess the situation. He should have come by to inform you of this."

"Yes, he should have," Givon stated. "Bikers?"

"Yes. Clark works organized crimes."

"Do you happen to know the name of the biker?"

"Sorry, Sheriff. I don't. Clark hasn't reported in."

"Isn't that unusual?" Givon asked.

"Not if he's in the midst of investigating a known outlaw biker gang."

Givon didn't agree with that at all and this was turning out to be a whole lot more complicated than just a burned-out car. Except now, he knew the first person he was going to question.

"If and when you get in touch with your detective, Captain, would you have him give me a call?"

"Will do, Sheriff."

* * * *

Givon waited by his truck, standing on one of the Laramide uplifts overlooking the Wind River Basin. It was one of the most beautiful places on Earth and he considered himself fortunate that this was where he'd grown up. The sound of another vehicle coming up the narrow single road had all his senses on high alert.

The truck came to a stop and the engine turned off. A door slammed and Givon turned his head as North Tabion walked up to him. North intimidated people. The air around him practically vibrated with authority and his blue eyes were cold enough to freeze fire. A bandana hid most of his blond hair. Givon saw his reflection in the man's mirrored sunglasses.

"You rang?" North drawled in a deep gravelly voice. It matched his outward persona. A Red Wolf strip encircled the bottom of his leather cut while dark jeans and a white T-shirt hinted at the muscles under his big frame. A chain for his wallet attached to his belt and tattoos peeked out from under one sleeve.

"I've got a Cheyenne detective somewhere in my jurisdiction inquiring about a woman who was allegedly beaten up by a biker," Givon said without preamble.

"The hell you say?" North grumbled.

"What the fuck is going on, North?"

"Who's this detective?"

"I don't know," Givon said with a frustrated sigh. "I called his captain and he hasn't heard from his guy either. So let me tell you what I have—a report on a woman being beaten, bikers are involved, my department's on the take and a burned-out car belonging to a woman named Merrie Walden. Does any of this ring a bell?"

"Fuck," North muttered. "It's not us, man. I swear it."

"Well if it's not you then it's the Demon Devils."

"The double Ds are scum," North told him. "There's no love lost between us and them."

"I know that. Can you keep your ears open? Let me know if you hear anything?"

"Sure," North said. "You know I'm trying to turn the gang around. Most of us don't want to stay on this outlaw path. That's why they voted me into the presidency when Old Patch died."

"I know," Givon said quietly. "And I'm glad. I've always hated us being polar opposites. You're still my best friend."

North gave him a playful shove on the shoulder. "Don't get all mushy on me. My dick doesn't do men."

"Asshole," Givon swore as he turned to stomp back to his truck. "Doing me would rock your world. Make you immune to the charms of women. But hell if I want that kind of commitment from you, you pervy bastard."

"Love you too," North called out and then laughed.

Givon flipped him off as he started his own truck. He maneuvered around North's, leaving his friend behind. They'd grown up together, both victims of abusive dads, leaning on each other to survive the horrors. Once they'd hit high school, they began going in different directions. Givon had been determined to become a cop so he could put men like their fathers' behind bars while North had started hanging out with the local biker gang, the Red Wolves.

Even with all the bullshit between an outlaw gang and the police, they'd managed to maintain their friendship, although very few people knew they were still talking to each another. And when North had come to him earlier in the year — after he'd become the gang's new president — to tell him that the Red Wolves were going legit, Givon had given him all his support.

He felt better talking to North, knowing his friend didn't have a thing to do with the trouble involving Merrie Walden. Now it was time for him to talk to the other biker gang.

North waited for Givon to drive away before pulling out his phone. He hit a number and listened until the call went through.

"Yeah, Boss?" Draven, his VP, asked.

"Meet me at the Demon Devils' bar on Route 18."

"Trouble?"

"Always with those bastards."

He hung up and headed toward his truck. His truck was old and he wanted to preserve it for as long as possible. As he made his way out of the mountain pass and back onto the road, he thought about whom he could contact to find out what the Devils had been up to lately.

Sometime later, he saw Draven's bike parked on the side of the road hidden within the tree line. It was the typical place they used when they wanted to spy on the other club.

Draven dismounted his bike and walked over to North's passenger door, hopping into the truck with ease.

"What's going on, Boss?"

"I think we have a big fucking problem on our hands," North said grimly.

"If it involves the Demon Devils, I'm not surprised. They've been a big fucking problem for the past twenty years."

"They beat up a woman and implicated Givon's office, stating it's on the take."

"Givon's office is *not* on the take."

"I know that and you know that, but if the Internal Affairs Bureau gets wind, Giv's job could be on the line and the Wolves have come too far to let some investigation bullshit fuck everything up. Now, who do we have who can get us some Intel on what they're doing?"

"Reaper's at Rawlins," Draven said. "I think the Devils have a few guys on the inside. Could stage an interrogation."

"I don't want Gray Dog getting wind that I know anything."

"You know how prison is, Boss—lots of alone time."

North nodded. "I want you to handle this personally, Draven. Givon's my best friend, although only you know that."

"I hear you, Boss. I'll head out to Rawlins now. I should just make visiting hours."

"Good."

Draven exited North's truck and headed to his bike. The man roared out on his run. North would be damned if he let anyone fuck up what his club had worked so hard to achieve. If the Demon Devils wanted another turf war, then he was going to be prepared.

Chapter Fifteen

The next two days were miserable for Merrie. During the night, she stared up at the dark ceiling, replaying over in her head the night they'd all been together. What had she done wrong? What could she say to fix this? Her nerves stretched thinner and thinner each hour. Leo tried to keep her mind off Braden but it was like walking on a tightrope.

During the day, she continued working with Leo at the office. Whenever he was called away on emergencies, she stayed behind and took calls, made appointments and cleaned and stocked the exam rooms. She managed to stay busy and on the occasion Braden crept into her thoughts, she'd log on to the Internet.

On a hunch, she typed the Demon Devils in the browser. It surprised her when she found a website for them. At the top, it proclaimed their club name and their logo entwined double Ds. She clicked on the chapter link and realized that the Destiny branch was only one part of the whole Demon Devil world. There was also a photo section and she brought that up, scrolling through until she saw the gray-bearded man from that night.

Her heart began to pound fearfully and she broke out into a cold sweat. Merrie grabbed a pen and paper and wrote down his name—Gray Dog. She right clicked on the picture and sent it to the printer. It may only be black and white but at least she'd have something tangible. She scrolled through all the pictures, unable to find Axe.

Merrie dug Detective Christianson's card out of her back pocket. She'd been carrying it around all the time, just in case. She dialed the cell number from the landline but all she got was his voicemail so she left a message for him to call her. Just finding Gray Dog's picture brought it home that what had happened was *real* and she couldn't sweep it under the rug. She couldn't forget about it. Now that she was mostly recovered and had had time and distance from the event, the memories weren't so painful to think about.

She clicked back to the home page and studied the website for a moment before going back to the browser and bringing up the FAQs. The questions started out standard, ones she would've asked. *What does MC stand for? What do the colors stand for? Is this a gang?*

The fourth question was about the logo and its significance upon the leather vest, also known as a cut. The colors and the two Ds were the club's insignia, a way to identify them to other clubs or bikers in the area. Every cut was the same because the placement of the name, the logo and charter chapter were all important. The one percent stitched into the leather designated that they were outlaw, made famous by a 1948 statement by the American Motorcycle Association that ninety-nine percent of motorcyclists are good people enjoying a clean sport and only one percent are antisocial barbarians. Something nagged at the back of her mind, but it was so elusive she couldn't focus on it.

Feeling drained, she clicked off the Internet and shut the computer down and folded the printed picture up to slip it in her back pocket, along with the detective's card. When she looked at the clock, it startled Merrie to see it was close to six p.m. Leo still hadn't returned, so she closed up, putting the phones on service call and setting the alarm. The office was half a mile from the farmhouse so she took off walking, enjoying the crisp evening air.

When she reached home, Braden's truck sat in the driveway and lights shone in the kitchen. She walked softly up the steps and over the porch to open the door. She heard Braden on the phone and stopped when he said her name.

"Why can't you pick Merrie up?" Braden demanded, his tone harsh and slightly confrontational. "Damn it, Leo, you're driving me up a wall. I can't be around her—you know that. I don't know. There's a room above the barn I can use. I'll move in there for the time being, give you both a chance to work things out. No. I said no, Leo." He paused for a moment, as if listening to the person on the other end, then continued, "Yeah, yeah."

He hung up so she decided it was safe to walk in. Her heart hurt and all she wanted to do was cry. How could the one beautiful night they'd had turn into something so bitter?

The screen door slammed behind her and she put her keys onto the foyer table where she kept them. Braden stepped from the kitchen.

"I was going to come and get you," he said.

She shrugged. "I'm here now." She headed to the stairs. "I'm going to shower."

She hurried upstairs away from him, away from the tension that hung thick in the air. Once inside the bathroom and she had the shower to mask sound, she sat on the toilet and cried.

She couldn't stay. That much was clear. She was just a girl—no one important—and she refused to be *that* girl, the girl who broke up Braden's and Leo's brotherhood. No matter what she felt for them, no matter how much it hurt, she would have to leave. She couldn't—wouldn't—ruin their relationship.

As steam from the shower she wasn't using filled the room, she tried to think about what she was going to do. First and foremost, she needed money. She'd never thought to ask Leo for her wages since she considered working as a way to thank both of them for their help. But she figured he wouldn't mind either giving or lending her some cash. She also needed to get her driver's license replaced but decided to wait until she went to Cheyenne.

A wave of sadness swept over her. Already she was missing this house, this ranch—missing Braden and Leo. In the couple of weeks she'd been there, she'd grown to love the land, the view of the mountains and the simple way of life. She had enjoyed cooking in the big kitchen, feeding her men. She thought she'd finally found a home and now she had to leave it.

She should be used to saying goodbye. She'd done it too many times in her life.

Merrie wiped her cheeks. She'd survive. She'd spent her whole life surviving, so she knew moving on wouldn't kill her. Perhaps one day she'd harden her heart and realize that happily ever after wasn't in her cards. Girls like her weren't meant to have the perfect home and the perfect life.

She took a quick shower, mindful of the cast on her wrist then turned the water off. She wrapped a towel around herself, grabbed her clothes and headed into her room. Halfway there, she found Braden's door open. She couldn't help but peek. His pillow and blanket were gone, and his closet door stood open. She knew without checking further that Braden had already left for that room above the barn.

She continued to her room and closed the door with a soft click. Then she put on her nightshirt and a pair of clean panties before towel-drying her hair, all the while figuring out how to ask Leo for some cash so she could leave. The sooner the better, so Braden could have his life back.

Chapter Sixteen

Givon's personal cell phone vibrated at his hip and he reached absently for it, glancing quickly at the caller ID.

"Hey," he greeted.

"I have an anonymous tip for you," North told him.

"The whole purpose of anonymity is that I don't fucking know you," Givon stated.

North chuckled. "You want this tip or not?"

"Sure."

"Have you interviewed the Devils yet?"

"No," Givon said. "I've been waiting for this damn Cheyenne detective to call me so I don't go in blind, but no one's heard from him."

"Sounds like there's a lot going on in your jurisdiction that you don't know about."

"Fuck you," Givon grumbled.

"You wish. Listen, you'll want to talk to Gray Dog. He's the president of the Demon Devils."

"I know who he is. Why him specifically?"

"There's a rumor he gave the order to burn the car."

"And how did you happen to get this piece of gossip?"

"Now I can't reveal my sources, Sheriff. It's anonymous."

"And I also know there's a bitter feud between the Wolves and the Devils. How do I know this isn't just a pissing contest?"

North snorted. "Come on, Giv. Those assholes moved into our territory. This is Wolf land."

"Actually, this is my land," Givon said sharply. "You break the fucking law, North, and I'll be on your ass like flies on shit. Hear me?"

"I hear you. We're cool, Sheriff. And the tip is good. Talk to Gray Dog—aptly named. He's got a long gray beard and he smells like a dog. You can't miss him."

The call went dead and Givon slowly replaced his phone. He sat for a moment thinking, contemplating what to do, when he decided to go with his gut. He rose and headed out of his office to Jack's desk.

The office was large enough that he was able to give each of his deputies a desk. The jail was an extension of the office. There weren't many crimes committed in Destiny to warrant a bigger jail somewhere else. There was one general cell and a smaller one with actual walls for isolation. Presently, only Jack was in, since Givon had one deputy following up on a robbery and another directing traffic because of a downed light.

"I'm going to interview the Demon Devils," he told the deputy.

"You want me to go with you?" Jack asked eagerly.

Givon shook his head. "Man the phones. When Sandy gets back, you can head to lunch."

"You sure?"

"Yeah. See you later."

* * * *

When Givon stepped into the dark interior of the Demon Devil's bar, he felt twenty pairs of eyes zero in on him and all of them hostile. The two prospects holding court at the door followed him in, standing silent as he looked at each man, showing he wouldn't be intimidated nor would he back down from anyone. Finally, his gaze landed on the president of the club, Gray Dog, who stood behind the bar with hands spread on the countertop.

"What can I do for you, Sheriff?" Gray Dog boomed through the darkened, hazy interior of bar.

Givon continued forward but kept his hand near his revolver. It was like entering into a nest of vipers and he prepared for any one of them to strike.

"Just here to ask a question or two about a burned-out car that was found at the county line," Givon replied smoothly. He kept his gaze on Gray Dog's eyes, to see if he showed any flicker of recognition or response of any kind.

"I don't own a car," Gray Dog replied. "In fact, I don't think anyone here owns a car. Does anyone own a car?"

A chorus of "no" echoed through the room.

"The car belonged to a woman named Merrie Walden. Does that name ring any bells?"

Gray Dog shook his head. "Nope." Again, he looked around to his men. "Do any of you know this woman?"

And like before, a chorus of negative responses sounded—not that it surprised Givon. Bikers were a tight knit group of people, thick as thieves, which was more than apropos in this situation.

"Well, Sheriff," Gray Dog said. "Looks like we don't know nothing, so why don't you get back to your comfy sheriff's chair?"

Givon looked around once more. "And you have an alibi for two Friday's ago?"

"I've got about fifty," he said smugly, gesturing around the room. "I serve the drinks and Friday is one of our busiest nights."

Givon decided to play a little bluff. "I've got a witness who places Merrie Walden here."

Gray Dog narrowed his eyes. "I'd be mighty interested in meeting this so-called witness because he or she is a lying fuck."

"You're just a law-abiding citizen, eh, Mr. Lester?"

"I even pay my taxes, Sheriff."

"Of course," Givon murmured. "Well, if you hear of anything, please to let me know."

"Sure thing," Gray Dog replied. "You'll be the first person I think of."

Givon heard the insincerity in the man's words and the mocking laughs of the club members just verified the president's pretense. He nodded, turned on his heel and proceeded toward the door. One of the prospects opened it for him and all but booted him outside as it banged shut behind him.

* * * *

Givon stomped through his office, his boot heels loud on the wooden floor. Jack filled out a report and Sandy worked at her desk. The woman kept his office running with military precision. Occupied with a phone call, she reasoned with someone on the other end of the line so he didn't wait, just headed into his office and closed the door. As he approached his desk, a few small details seemed out of place. Some papers had been disturbed. A folder lay crooked. He eased into his chair, scanning all around. The side drawer on his desk sat cracked open. Not much, just a little, but it was enough to let Givon know someone had been searching through his stuff.

He opened the drawer and saw that his report notebook was there. He knew exactly what was inside, random notes he'd jotted down after speaking to Braden McClintock and Leo Cloud Dancer.

Givon got up from his desk and marched back into the lobby. Sandy finished her call and Jack looked at him.

"How long have you both been back?" he questioned.

"Um...twenty minutes?" Sandy answered, looking at Jack, who nodded. "As soon as I got back, Jack ran to get a sandwich but he ate at his desk."

"Did anyone go into my office?"

She shook her head. "Not that I know of. Jack?"

"No," Jack said quickly. "Why?"

"Someone went through my desk."

Their eyes widened.

"Wait a minute," Jack said. "I went to the restroom right before Sandy returned and when I got back, a man was here."

"What did he want?"

"I don't know," he replied. "He seemed high or stupid or something. Said his neighbor killed one of his chickens but that was as far as I got. When I asked the man who he was, he called me a dumb shit and stormed out of here."

"And you didn't recognize him?"

Jack shook his head. "I've never seen him before. If he was messing around your desk, he was probably looking for money."

Something about that statement just didn't sit right with Givon. He didn't want to believe that his office was corrupt but he couldn't ignore his gut tightening as he stared at Jack's innocent baby face.

All he could do was nod as if he believed him, making sure to keep his face blank.

"Okay. If you see him around town, you let me know."

Damn it! He hadn't believed anyone in his office was on the take. But he'd learned over the years to listen to his gut instinct when it started honking like a damn trumpet. He made a mental note to do a more thorough background check on Jack when his phone rang.

"Sheriff Halloran," he answered.

"Sheriff, this is Detective Clark Christianson," the man greeted. "I believe you've been trying to contact me."

"Ah, yes," Givon replied. "I was surprised when I discovered you'd been organizing an investigation in my jurisdiction without the courtesy of a call."

"Part of the report, Sheriff, is an accusation that your department might not be as law abiding as possible."

Indignation burned through Givon but he held back on voicing his anger. Then he thought about a way to verify the whereabouts of Merrie Walden.

"Miss Walden was perfectly fine talking with me," Givon replied blandly.

A slight pause followed.

"You've...talked with her?" Detective Christianson asked.

"I did. How else do you think I got your number?"

"I must say, that's surprising to hear. I was adamant with her and Mr. McClintock to call me if you came by."

A sliver of satisfaction coursed through him. "Because I might be untrustworthy?"

"To keep her safe."

"If that's true, then what are you planning to do with the Demon Devils?"

"Shit," the detective muttered. "How much do you know?"

"Not everything. Otherwise, I wouldn't have had to call your captain to hunt you down."

"Stay out of this, Sheriff, or I'm going to have to place a call to Division of Criminal Investigation. Wouldn't want the DCI breathing down your neck, would you?"

"Is that a threat, Detective?"

"It's a reminder that you're not being portrayed as squeaky clean in this mess, okay?"

He clicked off, leaving Givon obsessing over that last sentence. Why would a detective from Cheyenne call Merrie Walden's case a *mess*?

Chapter Seventeen

Merrie didn't know what woke her up later that night, but one minute she slept soundly and the next moment she snapped her eyes open. She lay on her side, facing the window. The wind whipped the branches on the tree by the panes. A storm brewed, evident by the rumbles of thunder rolling across the land.

Perhaps that's what had woken her. She tried to calm her racing heart, but her nerves vibrated with unease. Something was wrong. She didn't know what it was—only that something was not right in the house. The glowing clock face showed it was close to two in the morning, so she sat up and listened intently.

Cautiously, she rose and slipped on her pants and slippers before going to the door and easing it open. Her heart thundered heavily, even though she didn't know why. Something just seemed...off.

Storm clouds occluded the moonlight so she moved cautiously down the hallway, feeling her way along. Part of her felt like a fool for being scared. Then she heard a footstep downstairs and the hair rose on the back of her neck. She hurried to the bathroom since it was closest to the stairs and slipped behind the door. The crack where the door hinged provided her a peephole. It was dark, but a moment later, a shadow crept up the stairs until it reached the top, where it hesitated. It first went to Braden's bedroom and opened the door. Next, it moved farther down the hall. As it drifted from her line of sight, she quietly tiptoed around the door to the stairs and flew down them, staying as silent as possible. Her hands shook and she breathed so shallowly, she feared she might pass out. The only thing that saved her was the knowledge that if she did faint, then the bad guy upstairs was going to get her.

There was no other conclusion except that he was there to hurt her. She didn't know where Leo was and Braden had gone to the barn, so all she had was herself to rely on. Merrie picked up her keys, being sure not to make a sound. As quietly as possible, she opened the front door and dashed out into the night. The only place she knew of to be completely safe, was the office. Leo's office could be barricaded, shutting her inside with all the bad guys locked out.

Leo's truck was gone. That fact barely registered in her brain before she started sprinting down the driveway. Once she got to the edge of the property, she ducked into the tree line and used the darkness as cover. Her heartbeat roared in her ears as her fight-or-flight response urged her to run even faster. Unfortunately, her slippers weren't that great on the dew-slicked ground. The brewing storm swirled leaves around as she continued as quickly as possible.

Once there, she unlocked the door, her hand shaking so badly she almost dropped her keys. Then she hurried inside and reset the alarm before heading to the phone. She picked it up and hesitated. She didn't have anyone's cell number. And she couldn't call the cops. For all she knew, it might be the sheriff who had snuck into the house. So she decided to wait it out. She was safe, at least for now.

Merrie walked back to Leo's office and closed the door, locking it before huffing and puffing to move the credenza in front of it. No one would get in now. She sat on the couch and pulled the throw blanket around her shoulders just as she heard a mighty clap of thunder and the sound of rain hitting the roof. She lay on her side and let the sound, as well as the knowledge that no one was going to hurt her, lull her back to sleep.

* * * *

Braden heard his phone ring but he ignored it. When it rang the second time, he reluctantly picked it up.

"Yeah?" he grumbled.

"My emergency call was bogus," Leo practically shouted at him. "Get to the house and check on Merrie."

Braden sat up and shook his head, trying to clear away the lingering sleep. "What?"

"My emergency call!" Leo yelled. "It was a fake! I was called away from the house, leaving Merrie alone. Go check on her, Braden!"

Braden didn't even respond. He jumped from the uncomfortable single bed and grabbed his jeans. Seconds later, he sprinted toward his truck. Everything became a blur as the world narrowed into a single thought — Merrie was in trouble or Merrie could be hurt. If anything were to happen to her…

It seemed to take forever to get back to the house, although it was only a five-minute drive. Braden found the house dark. Foreboding. It had rained briefly, long enough to turn the ground muddy and slick. He jumped from the cab and ran up onto the porch. The first thing he immediately noticed was that the front door was unlocked. His heart gave a painful lurch but he tried to keep the panic at bay. As he stepped inside, he flipped on the entrance light and called out her name.

"Merrie! Merrie, where are you?"

Silence.

He ran upstairs to her bedroom. Her door stood open. Inside, he discovered her bed empty. He spun and began going through the whole house.

"Merrie!"

Quiet reigned.

He ran downstairs, almost sliding out of control when he reached the bottom. Braden headed into the back of the house where the laundry room was located and stopped dead in his tracks. The back door hung open and the gouged wood around the door lock, as well as a puddle of water inside the threshold, told the story.

Someone had broken in. Someone had come inside their home and Merrie was missing. The two images warred in his brain, causing fear to constrict his lungs until all he wanted to do was hit something.

Rocks crunch and sprayed as a set of tires slammed to a halt. Boots rang across the porch and a second later, Leo called out.

"Merrie! Braden!"

"Back here, Leo," he said, his voice sounding a little wobbly to his own ears.

The front door slammed shut behind him and a second later, Leo came to a halt next to him. "Where's Merrie?"

Braden pointed at the door. "Look. Crowbar marks."

"Shit!" Leo muttered. "Merrie?"

Braden shook his head. "Not here."

Leo pushed the door open farther and flipped on the back light. The earlier rain had erased any footprints.

"So this happened before the storm," Leo stated needlessly. "Do you think...Axe was here? That he took her?"

"I don't know," Braden growled as he stomped back toward the front door. Helplessness raged through him and he hated feeling so impotent. His mind raced in so many directions it had given him a headache. All he wanted was bury his face in Merrie's neck and never let her go. Dear God, what had possessed him to think he could just push his affections for her aside?

"The keys!" Leo cried. "Her keys are gone."

"The office." Braden took off running to his truck with Leo on his heels. Braden's heart hammered out hope. She *had* to be there! She just had to, because if she wasn't... Well, he didn't want to dwell on what that would mean.

Dread swarmed in his chest as he sped like a bat out of Hell, eating the half-mile distance as if it was nothing then skidding to a halt in front of the office. Leo jumped out and unlocked the door, barely managing to shut off the alarm as Braden pressed in after him.

Darkness shrouded the office. Silent. A tomb.

"Merrie!" Braden shouted.

Leo flipped on the lights before gesturing Braden to follow him. He hurried toward his office, Braden on

137

his heels. When Leo tried to open his office door, the doorknob wouldn't turn.

"It's locked," Leo stated. "I never lock this door." He spared a quick, hopeful look at Braden before banging on the door.

"Merrie! Are you in there? Open up. It's me and Braden."

The faintest noise penetrated through the thick wood then Merrie called out.

"Yes," she said, her voice muffled. "Wait. I moved your credenza in front of the door."

Relief poured through Braden, turning his knees weak. He had to use the wall to hold him up so he didn't collapse. Scraping and grunting followed then the lock clicked. As soon as the door swung open, he pushed Leo aside and swept her into his arms.

She stiffened, and for a moment, he thought she would push him away. But then she wrapped her arms around his neck and squeezed him as tightly as he was squeezing her.

"Oh, my God," he whispered in her ear. "I was so scared, Merrie. I'm sorry. I'm so sorry."

"Shh," she soothed. "You found me."

Braden let her go so Leo could hug her. She closed her eyes as she rested against his chest. Seeing her nestled in his brother's arms brought up a wealth of tender emotions in Braden, emotions he'd previously run from. But the thought that something could've happened to Merrie, that someone could've taken her from them, brought what really mattered into crystal-clear clarity.

"Did you see who it was?" he asked.

She shook her head. "I heard a noise and hid. I knew if I could make it here, I'd be safe. So I snuck out and ran."

He shared a dark look with Leo. Never again would they leave her alone, leave her defenseless. His stubbornness had almost gotten her hurt or worse — killed.

"Let's go home," he said.

She peeked at him. "All of us?"

He nodded. "Yes. All of us."

Leo turned off the lights and reset the alarm to lock up. Merrie sat between them and Braden reached out and linked his fingers with hers. He was done fighting a battle he was never going to win anyway.

When they got home, Merrie walked them through what had happened and how she'd slipped out, knowing the office would be the only safe place until both of them showed up. They searched the house and discovered nothing missing, so the only conclusion Braden could draw was the fact that the intruder had indeed been after Merrie.

They nailed the back door shut and locked the front door. Merrie took a table chair and jammed it against the doorknob. Braden knew she needed the security right now so he didn't say a word. And once everything was secure, he saw the relief sweep over her face.

"Are you going to be all right?" he asked.

"He knows where I am," she said. "I'm no longer safe."

"We'll figure this out," Leo replied, hugging her. "We should call Givon. He's the sheriff and he'll be able to help us find this man."

"How can we trust him?" she asked.

"We have to trust someone, Merrie."

She nodded. "Okay. I found a picture of the other man, the one with the long beard. And I called Detective Christianson but he never answered."

"We'll call again first thing in the morning," Braden affirmed. "But right now I need to tell you how sorry I am for my behavior. I was pushing you away because—"

She placed a finger over his lips. "It's okay, Braden. I get it. Yes, there is an age gap between us and I understand the hesitancy on your part. Even though I'm only twenty-three, I'm not a little girl."

"Believe me, I do know that." He took her hand in his. "When I thought something had happened to you, I...I panicked. I was afraid I wouldn't have the chance to tell you that I'm...I'm falling for you."

She smiled tenderly. "I know. I feel the same way."

"I'm scared," he whispered. "I'm afraid if I fall in love with you, you'll leave."

She encircled his waist with her arms and hugged him tightly. He had to admit that she felt good pressed up against him, as if she were a pillar of strength. And maybe she was, because she wasn't laughing at him. She wasn't running away. She might be tiny compared to him, but she had more strength than anyone he knew.

"I'm terrified too," she admitted softly. "Panicked that you'll push me away before I can prove that my age is just a number. It doesn't define who I am or what I want."

"What *do* you want?" he asked huskily.

"You—and Leo." She looked at his brother. "Both of you. I realize this is unconventional and illogical, and hell, probably impractical, but there's not a way to separate both of you from my heart."

Leo leaned over and kissed her lightly on the mouth. "Let's go with the illogical. The impractical. The unconventional. Tam Apo is wise in his judgment."

Merrie took his hand and—while still holding onto Braden—began walking with them to the stairs. Her toffee-colored eyes shone with love, with a hint of wickedness shining through. Braden thought she was the most beautiful woman he'd ever seen and willingly followed her.

Chapter Eighteen

Braden placed his hand behind her neck and pulled her to his body. She rested her hands on his chest, feeling his heat burning through his shirt, his muscles rippling with every breath he drew. Leo moved in behind her, effectively sandwiching her between their two rock-hard bodies. Have one in front of her and one behind her rendered Merrie thoughtless. Before she could gather her wits and process what was happening, Braden swooped down and covered her mouth with his.

As he probed her mouth with his tongue, an electrical current charged throughout her body. Voracious, he took everything she had to give and demanded more. Her juices leaked between her legs as need pumped hot and heavy through her blood.

Leo slid his hand around her to unbutton and unzip her jeans. He smoothed her pants over her hips then tugged her panties down. She wiggled her hips to help him. Bending, he took her shoes off and helped her step out of the ring of her clothes, leaving her naked from the waist down. Braden continued kissing her but he had to break away when Leo pulled her T-shirt up. Seconds later, her bra joined the pile of discarded clothing.

She couldn't help moaning when Leo brushed his fingers through the curls around her pussy lips. She knew she was already wet. Just the thought of her two men making love to her urged her juices to overflow. Leo made an appreciative growl when he discovered how wet she was.

Braden broke the kiss and stepped back. He undressed, maintaining eye contact with her. First he teased her with his shirt, unbuttoning it slowly. The material slipped down his arms, billowing slightly as it fell. He pulled his boots off before working on his pants. Good Lord, the man was giving her a heart attack with his little strip-tease. By the time he bared his cock, all she wanted to do was lick him.

As she readied herself to do just that, he spun her around and she was forced to watch Leo do the same disrobing show—lust torture times two. Leo climbed onto the bed then beckoned to her with his index finger. She obeyed, following him on hands and knees over the mattress.

Braden's hand on her head alerted her to what he wanted her to do. Happily, she bent forward to engulf Leo's cock with her mouth. The position thrust her ass out and Braden positioned her legs a little wider. Movement on the bed jostled her slightly then Braden settled his head between her legs and started licking her.

Dear heavenly God! She straddled his face as he made a feast of her. Leo kept thrusting his cock slowly, gently, into her mouth and he held her face still as he face-fucked her. She loved giving head, loved having the power over a man, but she'd never been in this position before of giving and getting at the same time. Her brain and body sailed into euphoria as she let Leo take control. Still, she managed to use her tongue over his sensitive shaft, kissing the hole as she sucked him in.

Braden pulled her clit into his mouth at the same time he found her pussy opening with his finger. He teased inside as he rubbed his thumb to her sensitive clit, causing her to moan around the hard dick in her mouth. Leo shivered at the vibration and picked up the pace, fucking her mouth with quick jabs.

There was no way she was going to last. Her orgasm rose, breaking over her like a tidal wave hitting the shoreline. Pleasure burst, flushing through her body, and she convulsed around Braden's mouth and finger. Before she drifted down from her high, Braden withdrew. He tore open a condom packet then he rose against her ass, holding her hips as he held his cock to the entrance of her pussy. She was so wet that his cock, so large and heavy, filled her immediately.

As he pressed into her from behind, he pushed her head forward more firmly on Leo's cock. Leo leaked heavily in her mouth and she hungrily slurped him up, loving his taste.

"Oh, yes," Leo moaned. "Suck me down deep, Merrie. Take it all."

She welcomed the dirty talk. It brought another orgasm to the surface. Tingles began to flow through her as she climbed higher and higher. She let out a squeal and arched her back, her cream running.

"Merrie," Braden gasped. "Oh, God, you're so tight."

"Fuck her, Braden," Leo ordered. "Fuck her, hard."

"Oh yes," Braden exclaimed.

He pumped big cock quickly now. His balls slapped her ass with each stroke.

Leo exploded first. He pushed deep into her mouth, holding her head still. He tensed just before his hot cum shot down her throat. After the second load, she thought she might choke, but swallowed as much of the sticky fluid as she could, although some of it dribbled out the side of her mouth.

When Leo was done, he let go of her head and fell back to watch Braden pound into her. His brother's release must have sent Braden over the top. He began grunting as his sweat trickled down his body to drip onto her. She loved feeling him come undone — this man who seemed so strict and unyielding. A wet, slurping noise accompanied the heavy slaps of him thrusting into her.

Leo ran his hand down her hip and over her pelvis to slip inside her curls and find her clit. It only took two light rubs to make the world explode a third time for her. She cried out and convulsed around Braden's shaft as he pushed it into her. His cock swelled as he exploded with a deep, hoarse cry. Spurt after spurt shot into the latex barrier, and he shuddered as he collapsed across her back, breathing heavily.

As Braden left her body, Leo wrapped her in his arms and lay back. Braden crawled into the bed and curled behind her, slipping his arm around her waist and burying his face against the back of her neck.

Chapter Nineteen

Merrie had to do something while they waited for Sheriff Halloran to arrive, so she decided to cook. Even though they'd already had breakfast and lunch was still two hours away, her stomach needed something besides nervous acid to churn on. So she made pancakes. Things were always better with lots of butter and maple syrup. She had a momentary vision of Leo and Braden covered in the gooey, delicious mess.

When Braden stepped into the kitchen to check on her, she shook her head to clear it. She knew both men were keeping an eye on her and she appreciated their thoughtfulness. They hadn't talked about last night yet, and although it had been the second time they'd all shared a bed, the emotions were completely different this time around. Leo had asked if she was theirs and yes, she was. But if a psycho was hunting her... She couldn't really commit when he was hunting her.

Finally, after she'd produced a stack of golden brown goodness, she heard a truck in the driveway.

She put the batter down and turned off the stove then carried the plate of pancakes to the coffee table and set them down before retreating to the opposite wall. She trusted Braden and Leo's judgment that they could trust Sheriff Halloran, but she was still jumpy after last night's visitor.

She barely remembered him from before. She'd forgotten how powerfully his light green eyes contrasted with his cropped black hair. Instead of the standard brown uniform, he wore a white button-down shirt tucked into very tight jeans, revealing a nice physique. The gold badge pinned on his chest twinkled at her and he gave her a respectful nod as he entered the house.

"Ms. Walden," he greeted in a deep voice. "It's nice to see you again."

Merrie nodded. "Hello, Sheriff. I made pancakes."

She gestured to the coffee table. He glanced at them, a little perplexed, and nodded his thanks. Belatedly, she realized most people would've offered coffee.

"We had an intruder," Braden said, getting right down to business. "They broke in through the back door, but the rain washed away any tracks."

Sheriff Halloran frowned. "May I see?"

For the few minutes that Braden had taken him to the back door, Merrie let her shoulders slump. She hated feeling this tense. It was beginning to give her a headache.

"It's okay," Leo murmured.

She flashed him a grateful smile. Leo was her sympathizer while Braden was her brawny defender.

When Braden and the sheriff came back, she sensed the lawman staring at her. She met his gaze steadily.

"I think this is partially my fault," Givon muttered. "Someone rifled through my desk and went through the notes I made about my visit here. I didn't want to believe someone could be a mole in my office but this can't be a coincidence."

"Shit," Braden muttered. "Do you know who?"

The brackets around the sheriff's mouth deepened with his irritation. "I think it might be one of my deputies, as much as it pains me to say it. He had this story of a man being in the office when he went to the restroom that sounded like total bullshit. Now, hearing about what happened last night, I can't get it out of my head."

He ran an agitated hand over his hair.

"Then I suppose he really does have the cops in his pocket," she murmured.

"He doesn't have *this* cop in his pocket," Sheriff Halloran stressed.

Warmth settled in her face. "Of course. I'm sorry."

The man sighed. "No, *I'm* sorry. I just can't believe this. Can you tell me from the beginning, Miss Walden, what's going on? It's been very difficult to talk to Detective Christianson."

"Same with us," Braden muttered.

"Let's sit," Leo said. "This is a long story. Pancake?"

"Er, no," the sheriff replied as he sat on the couch. Merrie decided to keep standing, since it helped to her focus. A sense of detachment formed from what had happened, as if it was some other girl's nightmare.

She told the story, keeping out the minor details, painting a stark black-and-white picture. She watched Givon Halloran's face change from concern and anger then eventually fading into the detached look that most cops adopt as they analyzed the information in their heads.

Leo brought the camera over to him and the sheriff scrolled through the pictures, his face grim looking.

"And I have a picture of one of the men," she said. "I'll be right back."

She ran upstairs then searched for her jeans from yesterday, pulling out the photo she'd printed from the website. When she returned to the men, she handed it to the sheriff. He unfolded it and turned around to look at everyone.

Merrie pointed to the man in the back. "This is one of the men."

"That's Gray Dog," Givon said. "I questioned him yesterday but got nowhere, of course. MC's are notorious for sticking together."

"You think I should leave Destiny?" Merrie asked softly.

"No," Braden instantly refused.

"Absolutely not," Leo stated. "One of us will always be with you from now on."

"You can't be everywhere with me and now that Axe might know where I am, I don't want to put you and Braden in danger."

"Wait a minute," Givon interjected. "Did you say Axe?"

"Yes." She nodded. "The man who hit me was named Axe."

"I thought you said the Demon Devils hurt you."

"They did. At their bar on Route 18."

"Axe isn't with the Demon Devils. He's a Red Wolf."

"I don't know what that means."

"Oh, shit," Givon muttered. He pulled out his cell phone and held up a finger as he called someone. "Hey, it's me. I'm at the McClintock ranch and I need you to come immediately but don't tell anyone where you're going. No, come right now. It's about the Wolves. Oh, and I know I don't have to say this, but bring your cut."

He ended the call and slid his phone back into its clip holder.

"Who was that?" Braden asked.

"North. He's on his way." Givon looked at Merrie. "I think I know why Axe is after you, Merrie, but let's wait for my friend, North, before we talk any further."

"Okay. But why?"

"North Tabion is president of the Red Wolves Motorcycle Club," he told her. "It's a different club, built right across the county line to avoid pesky cop interference. North's a good man, so don't be frightened when he pulls up. Okay?"

She nodded.

Once again, she had the need to do something while she waited so she made coffee. When it was done, she poured each man a cup and handed them out, not even bothering to ask them if they wanted any. She rolled her head around her neck in an effort to ease of the tension.

The rumble of a motorcycle took her down memory lane, into the back of her car as she stared at the snake tattoo, fearing for her life. She wanted to run and hide but she caught the sheriff's eye and he gave her an encouraging smile, so she tamped down the flashback and waited.

The motorcycle's engine died. Boots thudded against the porch. Leo opened the door before North Tabion could knock. Merrie's first glimpse of the biker surprised her. She was expecting someone...dirty. Bearded. Someone like Gray Dog or Axe. Instead, she got a hottie with blond hair and sky-blue eyes. He wore an American Flag bandana around his head, a pair of black jeans, a black T-shirt with a leather vest that had various patches on it and a red stripe that ran around the bottom.

Braden gave him a welcoming nod and North acknowledged back. The manly gestures drove her up a wall.

"What's going on?" the biker asked, looking directly at the sheriff.

Givon Halloran looked at Merrie. "Tell him the story but this time, use all the names."

It slightly annoyed her had to go through that night one more time. Leo walked over to her and took her hand, squeezing it. Again, she recounted the events that had led up to her stopping at the Demon Devil's bar.

"I got out of my car and when I looked over, I saw two men shaking hands. I didn't think anything of it until I went to make my call and one of the men came up and slapped me. He asked if I was...let's see, he asked if I was an old woman or an old lady—or something like that—then he asked if I was a spy. I said no, that I was lost and just wanted to call the police to help me when the other man—the one with the beard you named Gray Dog—told Axe he had to take care of me—"

"Wait," North stated. "Did you say Axe?"

"Yes."

"What'd he look like?"

The image rose quickly and sharply in her mind. She'd never forget him as long as she lived. "He had a goatee, mean eyes."

"And what was he wearing?"

The biker asked his question with a menacing tone. She looked at the sheriff and he gave her another encouraging smile.

"I...I don't understand. He had a vest like yours—"

"Red band around the bottom?"

"Yes."

"Son-of-a-bitch!" North exploded, as he began pace the living room.

Merrie jumped and scooted a little behind Leo.

"This is why he's after her," Givon told North. "To stop her from telling you exactly what she just told you."

Thoroughly confused, Merrie wished someone would explain what the hell it all meant, why she was attacked and why Axe felt like he had to hurt her. When it looked like she wouldn't get her wish, she boldly took a step closer to both Givon and North. North raised an eyebrow as he looked her up and down.

"What was it that I saw?" she demanded. "Make me understand why this Gray Dog told Axe to make sure my body was never found."

"Motorcycle clubs use their colors to make their affiliation public to both fellow gang members and to our rivals," North told her. "In this case, that would be the Demon Devils. They moved into our territory twenty years ago and there's been a feud ever since. The Red Wolves' vest—or cut—are like mine. If Axe was wearing his and he was on the property of the Demon Devils shaking hands with their president... Well, that's treason. Wearing your colors in rival territory is either a threat or a declaration of war, so he should've removed them or they should've fucked him up. Colors and patches are sacred. That's why you need to be absolutely sure who you saw was Axe."

"Do you have a photo of him?"

North reached for his phone in his back pocket and scrolled through until he found what he was looking for. He held the camera out.

Merrie only had to take one quick look to know it was *him* — her tormentor.

"Yes," she whispered. "That's him. That's the man who wore that vest and who was shaking hands with this man."

She held up the picture of Gray Dog that she'd printed out. "I don't know anything about motorcycle gangs," she continued. "I didn't even know what I'd seen. This man of yours — this Axe — was going to kill me over something I wouldn't even have known how to put two and two together?"

"I'll take care of him for you," North vowed. "I promise you that. You're under my protection now."

She stared at him, studied his eyes. He may have been in a motorcycle gang, but the difference between what she saw in his eyes and what she'd seen in Axe's eyes was like night and day. Either this North Tabion was a magnificent actor or he really meant what he said.

Something eased in her chest. It wasn't much, just a tiny crack of hope that she could finally put the ordeal behind her. As she opened her mouth to comment, however, the sound of another vehicle pulling into the driveway distracted her.

"It's Detective Christianson," Braden announced.

"Who?" North asked.

"That Cheyenne detective I mentioned," Givon explained. "You've missed out on a lot. Apparently, so have I."

As soon as the detective entered the living room, his gaze landed on North. He did not look happy.

Givon stepped forward. "I'm Sheriff Halloran. Thanks for finally stopping by so I can meet you face-to-face."

"I've been busy, Sheriff," Detective Christianson said with a hint of sarcasm. "Who's this?"

He jerked his thumb in North's direction.

"North Tabion, President of the Red Wolves," Givon said. "We've discovered who Axe is."

The detective looked at Merrie. "You've been talking? I thought we agreed to keep this between us."

"That was before someone broke into our house last night," Braden stated. "Givon's not the only one who's been trying to reach you."

"So who's this Axe?" Christianson asked, ignoring him.

"He's my sergeant at arms," North answered. "As such, I'm asking you to leave this to me."

"Leave it to you?" Christianson snorted. "What? Biker justice? We all know what that means, Mr. Tabion—an unmarked grave somewhere in these mountains."

North stiffened. "Don't believe everything Hollywood spits out, Detective. I'm perfectly willing to bring Axe to you once my crew and I have stripped him of his MC privileges."

"I've been working organized and gang crimes for a long time," Christianson said, "which means I've heard a lot of bullshit in my life so forgive me if I don't fucking believe you."

North took a forceful step in his direction. Givon jumped in front of him and held his shoulders.

"Not now," Givon whispered.

"This is a club matter," North insisted in a low voice. "Axe is a traitor to the Pack."

"I know. And I understand, North. You hear me?" Givon insisted. "I respect that."

North stared at him then slowly eased back, nodding.

"Wait a minute," Detective Christianson said. "Are you saying this Axe has defected to another club? This is just a dispute over colors?"

"This is a dispute over loyalty," North corrected. "The Demon Devils moved into our territory."

The detective scratched his chin. "You're clubhouse is over the county line, though, isn't it? So technically, there isn't a jurisdiction boundary, is there?"

At the taunt, North curled his hands into fists. For an instant, Merrie thought the biker was going to deck the cop. But Givon placed a hand on North's shoulder, which seemed to diffuse some of North's tension.

"Regardless," the sheriff said. "Axe has to be brought in for questioning, and it's up to Merrie to press charges."

Suddenly, all eyes turned in her direction. What had she missed?

"Merrie," Braden said. "You need to press charges. That man has to pay for what he did to you."

She looked at each of them, helpless to make a decision. All she had wanted was to forget.

"What…what does that mean?" she asked, trying to stall.

"By pressing charges, you would be signing a complaint alleging Axe of violating the law," Givon explained. "And by agreeing to press charges, you are also agreeing to testify against him in court."

Testify? "You mean I would have to confront him. See him again."

Givon nodded. "Unless he confesses."

"He won't confess," North said. Givon glared at him.

"Do I do that now?" she asked.

"No," Givon said. "I have to bring him in for questioning first then you need to come to the station within twenty-four hours to press charges. Merrie, if you don't, he'll walk free and you'll spend the rest of your life looking over your shoulder."

"Okay," she whispered. "I...I need to think."

She saw he wasn't happy with her answer but he eased back and relaxed his stance.

"All right," he said. "You have twenty-four hours. Do you understand?"

"Yes," she replied.

He gave a single stiff nod then headed for the door. North followed him. Detective Christianson watched both men before he turned back to Braden, Leo and Merrie.

"I would advise against pressing charges," he said.

"What?" Braden said angrily. "You want her to just let this asshole get away with this?"

"Listen to me," the detective said, keeping his focus on Merrie. "I've worked organized crime for twenty years and in that time, I've seen the gauntlet of witnesses. An outlaw motorcycle gang won't hesitate to hurt you in any way possible to shut you up. Even if you run, they'll come after your loved ones. Gangs work through fear and intimidation but it's also a guarantee. Think long and hard, Miss Walden, before you go accusing a member of a crime."

The detective strode out of the house as well, leaving Merrie shaking in her shoes. She thought she was safe but it seemed the only way to make sure was to forget the incident had ever happened.

* * * *

"Let me handle this," North insisted again.

"I can't," Givon said. "Axe beat her, for God's sake. I've seen the pictures. He forced her to jump out of a moving car, breaking her wrist. If it wasn't for her quick thinking and her bravery, I'd be investigating a homicide."

"This is my problem," North insisted. "The club will handle Axe."

"You told me you were going legit," Givon said, keeping his voice low so no one could over hear him.

"I am."

"Then back me on this."

Frustrated, North ran a hand through his hair. "I have to tell the other officers. He's in charge of security for the club, for fuck's sake!"

"Then talk them into giving him to me."

Detective Christianson stormed out of the house. His glare landed immediately on Givon.

"You've interfered in my investigation," the man snarled.

"What investigation?" Givon demanded. "You never even contacted me."

"Your office is part of this fucking mess," the detective declared. "Accusations have been made against you —"

"I'm pretty sure I know who my leak is," Givon interrupted. "If the Department of Criminal Investigations comes to Destiny then I have nothing to hide."

"We'll see, Sheriff," the detective snarled. He turned his back and stomped to his car. A few seconds later, he roared away from the house with a furious spin of tires on the rocky driveway.

"What an ass," North remarked.

"I don't like that man," Givon admitted. "Come on. Let's go find Axe."

Detective Christianson angrily dialed his brother. Axe picked up on the second ring.

"North knows," he snapped. "They're on their way. Get the hell out of there and disappear or else the girl might press charges."

"Ah, you do care about me," Axe drawled.

"Fuck you. If she doesn't press charges, you won't get arrested and you don't mention my name. Once I retire, I'm done. Understand?"

He ended the call before his brother said another damn word. He was tired of this shit. His retirement was set to start on Monday, which left him three days. No fucking way was he going to allow his brother to screw this up. If Axe simply laid low, maybe disappeared from the Red Wolves altogether, then his problems would be solved.

As long as he got his health benefits then his brother could go drown in a fucking lake, for all he cared.

Chapter Twenty

For the first time in a long time, Merrie felt as though she could relax. No more wondering or worrying. Axe would be dealt with and all she had to do was decide if she was going to press charges.

Of course she would.

Wouldn't she?

Did she want him loose on the streets, able to get to her again? She knew North had said he'd deal justice but she didn't know if she could fully trust him to keep his word. Gangs stuck together and if push came to shove, Merrie didn't hold out hope that North would condemn one of his biker brothers.

"Have you ever ridden a horse?" Braden asked, startling her out of her musings.

"Yes," she said. She hadn't grown up in her hometown in rural Wyoming or worked on a dairy farm without learning how to ride a horse.

He smiled. "How about the three of us take a ride, enjoy the rest of the day before I have to go back to work?"

She shot Leo a quick glance, who nodded.

"That would be wonderful," she said.

Since she didn't have boots to wear, her sneakers would have to do. Braden drove to the barn then introduced her to a little mare named Sassy. Sassy's dark chocolate coat gleamed in the sunlight. She bobbed her head in a greeting and Merrie patted the soft white fur on her face. And the horse didn't just walk. She pranced.

"That's why her name is Sassy," Braden explained.

"I love her." Merrie stroked the mare's velvety nose. Sassy nudged her arm, clearly looking for a treat. "I didn't bring anything with me, sweetheart. Next time, okay?"

They saddled their horses then took off at a moderate pace across the rolling green hills. Destiny backed up to the Wind River Mountain Range, a part of the Rocky Mountains. It was a popular tourist destination of hiking, climbing and skiing, and Braden and Leo's ranch had an eastern view of the sweeping landscape.

"Wyoming's highest peak is Gannett," Braden told her, pointing into the distance. "It's about thirteen thousand eight hundred feet."

"Although there's about fifty mountain peaks in the Wind River Mountains at thirteen thousand feet," Leo cut in dryly.

Merrie laughed. "I must admit, even though I grew up in Wyoming, I didn't know all that much about the mountains, especially this range."

They rode across the flat grass, between the trees and over a little mound into their own private clearing. Nearby a river sped past, its water glistening in the bright sunlight. Merrie couldn't help but wonder if this was the same river she'd walked through during *that* night. It probably was. There weren't many rivers in the area. She shivered despite the warm sunshine.

The men dismounted and she followed course, loosely tying the reins on a low-hanging branch.

"This is a beautiful place," she said. "Peaceful."

"And secluded." A wicked little gleam in Leo's eyes hinted that he had something fun in mind.

"Oh?" she inquired, her heart skipping a beat. "And just what would we do all by ourselves to stay occupied?"

Leo pulled her into his arms and covered her mouth with his, kissing her long and deep. Her senses spun and she clung to him.

"Merrie," he moaned as he broke the kiss to lick his way down her neck. "Lean against Braden."

Braden brought his arms around her shoulders and trapped her back against his chest—not that she intended to get away. Leo loomed over her, staring into her eyes for a moment before he claimed her lips again, sliding his tongue into her mouth to dance with hers. As Leo cupped her breasts and rubbed them through her shirt, Braden shimmied his hands down the sides of her body until he reached her hips. She wiggled her ass against his hard cock and he nuzzled her neck, just as he unzipped her pants so he could slide his hands inside and under her panties. As soon as he touched her clit, she almost jumped out of her skin, moaning.

"You are so sexy," Braden murmured in her ear, his voice heavy with sexual need. "Sexy and beautiful."

"And ours," Leo added. "Right, sweetheart? You're ours."

With Braden to her back and Leo tormenting her aching breasts, Merrie could only whimper her affirmation. Yes, she was theirs, and they were hers—

and everything she'd ever wanted in life was finally within her grasp. A home filled with love plus not one, but two, wonderful men.

As Braden pushed his finger into her, and Leo pinched her nipples, she bucked her hips and wiggled, seeking something and going crazy when the men continued their ruthless assault on her senses. They teased her, revving her up little by little until she could no longer contain her climax. She exploded, riding Braden's fingers as Leo swallowed up her passionate cry of release.

"That's it," Leo breathed against her mouth.

She humped Braden's hand, her inner walls milking her orgasm for a few breathless moments. As she slowly filtered back to reality, Braden removed his hand from between her thighs but kept his hard body pressed against her back. Leo gave one last swipe with his fingers against her nipples before cupping her face to give her a light kiss.

Both men helped her undress and her clothes fell at her feet. "Turn around, Merrie," Leo ordered.

She obeyed. Now she stared up at Braden and she saw all the love, the tenderness and yes, even the lust shining from his eyes.

Behind her, Leo ran one hand over the curve of her bottom, down the back of her thighs then up between them to touch her intimately. He dropped to his knees level with her ass and nudged her legs apart. The stance gave him better access to her anus. With his thumb, he circled the tight ring of muscles there. She tensed but the pressure he applied caused her to squirm.

"Don't worry," Leo assured her. "I brought plenty of condoms and lube."

The soft noises of the picnic basket opening then closing teased her ears, and a second later, cool gel drizzled into her crack. She gasped. Leo smeared the lube on and around her anus, his feathery strokes soon heating her blood and causing her juices to run. Now slick, he pressed his fingers inward. He bent one finger, rubbing along the back wall of her passage to stretch her. Slowly, he breached her with another digit, widening her. The thrust and burn took her breath away.

"You're so gorgeous." Leo groaned. "So wet. Feel how wet she is, Braden."

During all this time, Braden had simply watched her reaction to Leo's ministrations, but now he teased down along her stomach and slid his hand through her curls. When he found her folds, he dipped a finger into her warmth.

"So wet," he agreed. "I want to fuck this pussy. Would you like that, Merrie? Would you like my cock buried in your tight little cunt while Leo discovers the delights of your ass?"

Merrie panted. Not only did the images turn her on, but the fact that Braden was saying them revved her higher.

She moaned. "Oh yes."

Braden dropped to his knees to kiss her belly button then licked his way south until he reached the apex of her thighs. He nudged them apart and a second later, he licked her and sucked on her clit. He pushed one finger into her wet pussy then began thrusting, back and forth, hitting her G-spot and driving her out of her mind.

Leo placed his finger at her back entrance, prepping for penetration by mimicking Braden's fingers pumping inside her pussy. Before she even realized what was happening, her body exploded into a thousand pieces, shattering her strength. Stars bloomed behind her eyes and dimly she heard the rustle of condom wrappers tearing open. She opened her eyes and saw Braden lie down on the grass, his cock swollen and hard. He held her hand to help steady her as she straddled him. She fisted his dick, locked gazes with him and slowly lowered herself. Since he was big, it took her a moment to adjust to his girth.

"I'm just going to make sure you're loose enough to take me," Leo said. He dripped even more lube on her anus before inserting his finger again.

"Oh!" She groaned. "Yes, it feels so good."

That seemed to be all the proof he needed. In the next instant, he removed his finger from her and adjusted her body, pushing her forward until she lay on Braden, her breasts flattened on his chest. Leo moved into position behind her and gripped her hips. As he slowly teased her rosette with the tip of his cock, Braden reached between them to rub her clit. The burning returned and Merrie held her breath, waiting for the sting of pain to give way to pleasure. She'd had anal sex before but it felt different with Leo. Better. Amazing. Braden pulled out of her a little to give Leo more room and pleasure and pain mingled inside her. A second later, Leo popped his cock through the tight ring and he slid home.

Merrie gasped, reveling in the feeling of being completely filled. Possessed. Consumed. She had no words to describe the sensations. It was beyond anything she had ever imagined.

Leo's breath tickled the back of her neck as he held her hips still.

"That's it, baby," he said. "You're so beautiful sandwiched between us."

"She's so tight, Leo," Braden said. "She's gripping my dick like a vise."

Merrie moaned. "I can't believe how much I love this. Oh, my God, please move. Both of you... Please take me."

Bucking his hips, Braden started their rhythms, but it took a moment for Leo to match Braden's pace. Merrie bounced between them, resting her hands on Braden's shoulders. Sweat rolled off their bodies as their hearts thundered in time together.

Merrie quickly realized being between two men took a little finesse. As one went in the other pulled out and Merrie knew they were spiraling together. In and out, in and out, Merrie wound tighter, tighter, tighter. Suddenly her climax hit and pleasure spiked through her brain as she cried out in abandonment.

"Not gonna last," Leo gasped from behind her.

Leo's cock swelled in her ass just before he found his release. His cock pulsed inside her as he poured his seed into the latex barrier. He leaned and rested his head against her back for a moment before extracting his softening member.

"Merrie." She opened dazed eyes to see Braden staring up at her.

He started thrusting harder, his gaze locked with hers. The pressure started to build again, little by little. Merrie knew what awaited her—the absolute euphoria of a mind-blowing climax. She chased it by grinding herself down onto Braden's cock.

"Yes," he panted, pumping his hips. "Yes, come for me. Come for me, Merrie."

"Uh!" The world tilted off its axis and she splintered into a thousand pieces. He shouted as he followed her, his cock jerking deep inside her.

She collapsed. He arms came around her, holding her for a long moment before he withdrew to tug off his condom. Leo snuggled into her from behind and they shifted until they all lay on their sides.

The sun warmed her naked body. There was something almost sinful about being naked outdoors. The cool breeze helped dry the sweat on their bodies. She propped herself up and looked at each man, who stared at her with lazy, contented smiles on their faces.

"Why are you content to share me? I mean, you're so concerned with me being younger when, in reality, it seems to me that you'd each find it easier to have separate relationships."

They both blinked at her.

Finally, Leo answered. "You're incredibly strong, Merrie. Shoshone prize three things—strength, honor and loyalty above everything. You have that in spades. I admire you. So if the woman I care for happens to also love my brother, then I'm content with sharing."

Braden more or less gave a grunt of agreement. She smiled and relaxed as if a weight had been lifted from her shoulders.

"My mother was a drug addict," she told them.

Their smiles slipped away.

She'd never really shared her whole past with anyone before but she wanted her men to know that she didn't have her head in the clouds. "And she was a whore too, which is how I came to be. By the time I was ten, I was taking care of myself. I learned how to install a deadbolt on my bedroom door and I also learned how to sneak money from her johns so I could eat."

"Jesus," Braden whispered.

"As the daughter of the local slut, I gained a reputation, even though it really wasn't deserved. When I turned sixteen, my mother died so I went to live with my great uncle. I started working two jobs — one at a diner and one at dairy farm. I never cared about school and barely graduated. My dreams have always been simple. And I know there's an age gap between us, but truthfully, I don't see it. My age is a number but it's not who I am."

Braden intertwined their fingers and brought her knuckles up to his lips, kissing them. Leo gripped her other hand.

"A soul-baring moment, eh?" Braden said with a rueful grin.

"Don't you think it's time?" Leo replied, nudging him.

"I don't like talking about some things."

"I know," Merrie said. "You must have loved Samantha a lot."

"I was young and *thought* I was in love," Braden corrected. "Samantha and I were high school sweethearts and got married as soon as we'd graduated. We both attended UW for two years. I wanted to learn about business management but Sam…? Sam wanted to pursue something more. She'd studied French throughout school and had dreams of living in Paris. I didn't understand it and forced her to give it up because she was my wife. I thought we shared a desire of owning a successful horse ranch and living our lives together. But that fantasy was mine alone."

Merrie kept quiet, watching the emotions play over his face.

"By the time she turned twenty-one, she'd come to the conclusion that she didn't want to live in rural Wyoming on a ranch. She wanted to be in a city. A year later, on my birthday, I got served with divorce papers."

"I'm so sorry, Braden," Merrie said.

"Nothing to be sorry about. We were just way too young to marry."

"And you thought I'd be the same," she concluded. "That I'd be just as flighty."

He nodded. "After the divorce, I only dated women who were older than me. You're the first younger woman I've come to care for."

"I may be young, but I've lived a hard life." She spread her fingers through his soft chest hair. "I may be putting the feminist movement back a few decades, but all I want is a home and to take care of my two men."

"Your men, huh?" Leo asked, a big smile on his face.

"Yeah," she challenged. "You got a problem with my claim?"

"No, ma'am." He tugged her down onto his chest.

"Good," she said just before Leo touched his mouth to hers.

A feather light kiss from Braden danced across the back of her neck and everything else was forgotten for a long time.

* * * *

They returned from their picnic and Braden stayed behind to take care of the horses, while Leo drove him and Merrie to the house. She took a shower and then went down to start dinner.

That night, Braden didn't return for dinner. She knew he'd gone through some monumental feelings that afternoon by letting go of the baggage that had held him a prisoner for so long. He had more in common with her than he'd realized.

She and Leo ate dinner and when they finished with their meal, he took the dirty dishes out of her hands and nodded to the front door.

"Go to him."

"Are you sure?"

"I had you to myself not too long ago, remember?"

"That was when Braden was being a prick."

He smiled. "I know. But there's one thing to understand about being in a three-way relationship. Some days it'll be all of us, some days you and me, and other times you and him. What we have is going to require a lot of work and right now, he needs you. I know my big brother. I'll take you to him."

"I can drive the one minute to the barn."

He frowned. "I don't want you to be alone. Look what happened the last time."

"But I'm not alone, am I. The barn is right there and you're right here. Besides, you have dishes to wash."

She kissed his cheek and headed out of the door, taking his truck keys and driving the short distance to the barn. As she entered the low-lighted area, the smell of hay, leather and horseflesh assaulted her all at once. It was a good smell, one she remembered from being on the dairy farm. Horses were a little different from cows, of course, and she liked the heady aroma.

Braden emerged from a stall and looked at her, eyebrows raised.

"What are you doing here?"

"You missed dinner," she said.

"Yeah. Sorry. Just...had things on my mind."

"Good things?"

He nodded. "I was saying goodbye to Samantha — finally. It's only been nineteen years."

She walked up to him until she stood as close to him as possible without touching. "Good. I meant what I said, Braden. You and Leo are mine."

He brought his hands down on her shoulders. "And you're ours," he answered firmly. "I just wanted you to be sure, because once I give you my heart, I won't ever want to let you go."

"Then kiss me, Braden, because I'm not leaving you, ever."

Braden slid his tongue into her mouth, twining it with hers, jolting a salacious moan from her. He explored each hidden corner of her depths, plunging in and out. Fire danced through her body from his kiss alone. He raised his left hand to hold her head immobile while he swept his right hand along her rib cage to pull her closer to his chest. She wrapped her arms around his neck and threaded her fingers into his hair.

When he finally broke the kiss and she looked up at him, blue fire shone from his eyes. "I want to continue this but I reek of horse."

"I don't care," she whispered and dragged his lips back down her hers.

As they kissed, he walked her backward but it wasn't until her back hit the barn wall that awareness came rushing back to her. Her pussy instantly drenched at the wicked intent she saw in his eyes.

"Fuck me, Braden," she ordered breathlessly. "I want you inside me so bad."

He kissed her almost savagely, as though he couldn't get enough of her — as if he wanted to devour her. He swept his tongue in, meeting hers, dominating her. He roamed his hands over her body, bringing her alive, sensitizing each nerve to sizzle. She tugged on his shoulders, at his clothes and nipped the skin on his neck.

She was careful of his dick pressing against the zipper as she eased it down. She reached inside and brought his cock out, enjoying its size and hardness in her hand. As she gave him a hand job, he shoved her bra up and sucked each of her nipples. Up and down, he trailed his lips along her skin, taking each bud with his teeth, biting just hard enough to elicit a gasp from her then sucking until she arched in pleasure. Back and forth, he repeated the same on each tip, until her head thrashed from side to side and she thrust her pelvis upward, inviting him closer.

While Braden played with her breasts, he ran his other hand down her body. He rubbed her sensitive clit while he found the entrance to her pussy with his index finger, dipping it inside to tease her.

"Please." She moaned and arched her back, shoving her breasts harder against his face.

He engulfed her right breast in his mouth while he began kneading her other one with his left hand, rolling the taut nipple between his fingers. Merrie threw her head back, tensing at the unbelievable sensations radiating up from her groin. Braden released one of her breasts and stroked down to her legs, pushing her jeans down until she was able to get one leg out of them. This allowed her to open her legs wide and fit his body between them. "There's a condom in my back pocket," he said as he broke free from her breasts. "In my wallet. Be a good girl and roll it on me."

Merrie slid her hand along his ass until she found the wallet in his pocket. She withdrew it then opened it, seeing some money and cards before finding the condom. She took it out, dropped the wallet then tore the foil open. Quickly, she rolled the rubber over his swollen cock. She pinched the tip, leaving enough room for his blast of cum, before giving his balls a loving squeeze.

"Christ, Merrie," he growled.

He leaned up to kiss her mouth again, but this time, when he swept his tongue inside, she captured it with her teeth and sucked. He wrapped her long hair in his fist, pulling her head back to expose her neck. Nuzzling her throat, he licked the salty skin.

"I'm going to fuck you against this wall."

"Oh, yes," she all but purred, rubbing against him.

Braden lifted her and she hooked her legs around his waist, the perfect position for him to slide into her pussy. With one hard thrust, he impaled her and they both moaned at the exquisite feeling—wanton and wicked. He backed her against the wall and began pounding into her. Merrie met his thrusts with sharp jabs of her pelvis again and again. She tried to draw him closer, tried to get his cock deeper. Sweat poured from their bodies, her breathing harsh, staccato.

She adored being with both men, but there was something so primitive in this joining that she knew she'd be wanting it again. With Leo, she had beautiful, and with Braden, she had intensity.

She fell first. She mewled as the dam burst and her cream ran. Her inner muscles milked the hard cock rooted deep inside her. Braden let out his own harsh groan as he climaxed with her, pouring himself into the condom.

"Holy fuck." His labored breathing echoed in the stall. "Screwing in a barn like I'm seventeen."

"Get used to living out your youthful fantasies," she warned with a smile and winked.

Chapter Twenty-One

The next day dawned very bright. Maybe it was Merrie's rose-colored glasses but the world seemed peaceful, beautiful. After their little tryst in the barn, Braden had followed her back and Leo had waited for them upstairs. They had showered separately and when they'd fallen into bed, both men had nestled her between them.

Merrie kissed her men awake then bounded into the bathroom to do her morning ablutions before heading to make breakfast. She couldn't seem to keep the smile from her face as she scrambled eggs, buttered toast and crisped the bacon. When Braden and Leo made it downstairs, she slid warm plates to them and placed coffee near their hands. Then she kissed each man on the cheek before sitting to eat too.

After breakfast, she put the dishes in the dishwasher and turned it on before running out the door to hop into the truck next to Leo. Braden waved at them and he took off toward the barns while she and Leo headed to the office. Several people waited for them and she hurried to open the office quickly, booting up the computer and turning off the night service as she greeted owners and their pets.

The morning stayed busy but as lunch approached, they had a breather.

"Do you want to come into the back with me? I'm just going to finish up some of these reports while I have a moment," Leo told her. He leaned down and kissed her on the lips.

"If I come into the back with you now, we'll miss hearing the next patient come in."

"I can close up early so we can play doctor." He wiggled his eyebrows suggestively at her.

Merrie just laughed and shook her head.

"Well, then, let me finish up then we can grab a bite to eat. Shouldn't take me long at all."

"That would be great," she said.

He walked out of the reception area and she admired his tight, firm ass encased in jeans. *Wowzer.* Butterflies flittered through her belly as she wondered if they would have enough time for a quickie during lunchtime. Just imagining him plowing into her on his desk made her pussy clench in anticipation.

At some point during the night, she'd made up her mind. She was going to press charges against Axe. Her new start in life was at her fingertips and all she had to do was have the courage to grasp it—and that meant not looking over her shoulder every day. With Braden and Leo by her side, she felt safe. Protected. And strong enough to face her fear—to face *him*.

When the last morning patient left, Merrie began entering all the payments info into the accounting ledger. The door opened and closed. Merrie turned to smile at the next patient when her gaze landed on Axe. Her smile died instantly and her gaze fell to the big black gun he held in his hand.

"Get up from your chair and come with me," he said.

She didn't immediately obey. If she went with him, she was dead. She'd be lost somewhere in the wilderness, her body never discovered, and all she could picture was Leo and Braden as they searched for her for the rest of their lives, hoping to rescue her. Keeping her gaze trained on the gun, she absently scribbled out one word on the paperwork, just in case she was going to have to tell them about her death from the grave.

"Stand up!" he snapped at her. "Else I'd hate to kill your Indian lover in front of you."

She began shaking her head but she saw him flick the safety off and level the barrel at her. She couldn't risk him hurting Leo and if Leo came through that door right now, thinking to rescue her, she knew Axe wouldn't hesitate to fire the gun. She rose and came around the counter to stand in front of him. Part of her wished Leo *would* come out and save her and another part of her hoped he didn't because she didn't want him hurt. The crazy glint in Axe's eyes told her was prepared to kill someone.

"You've fucked everything up for me, bitch," Axe said angrily.

"You know, I had no idea what I saw that night," she said, stalling. "All I wanted to do was forget, but you're the one who won't let me."

"So now it's payback."

"They're going to know who took me. You'll be the number one suspect. Do you think you can hide from the sheriff?"

"Halloran is a fucking joke," Axe said.

"Then North. He didn't seem like a fucking joke."

"I have one more shot to get what I want."

He grabbed her arm and jerked her in front of him, poking the pistol into her back, urging her to walk. Outside, a scuffed white van waited. There weren't even tags on it for identification. He marched her to the back and opened it, using zip ties to tie her arms together, although it was slightly tricky with the cast around her wrist. Then he backhanded her across the face and she fell with a sharp cry. He closed the van doors and she was once again a prisoner of Axe, the madman.

The engine rumbled to life and seconds later, the van roared away from the office. Tears leaked from her eyes. Would she see Leo and Braden again? What would they do when she didn't come back? Would they know it wasn't her choice, that she'd been forced? Somehow, she'd known this showdown was coming, had felt it in her bones when Sheriff Halloran had left to go arrest Axe. Her gut had told her that this man wouldn't go meekly along with an arrest.

They drove for a long time. At first, she tried to keep her wits about her and count if they went left or right, but her sense of direction — which was never good to begin with — combined with a lack of a window, grew majorly skewed. Finally, Axe stopped the van and turned off the engine. She heard him walk around to the back then the doors swung open. Sunlight poured inside and she blinked at the brightness.

Axe yanked her out. She stumbled to her feet and tried to run, but he caught her easily. It was then that she noticed a forest surrounded them. He'd parked in a small clearing that held nothing more than a hunter's shack. A sick sinking feeling settled in her stomach.

"You've ruined everything," Axe told her again, shaking her. "You've cost me an easy slide into the Demon Devil's gang."

"Why would you turn against your own club?" She really didn't care one way or another but the longer she kept him talking, the longer she had before he hurt her.

"They're going legit," he muttered, grabbing her arm and dragging her toward the hunter's shack. "North was voted in as president and started spouting off about going straight. He turned the other assholes of the club into pussies. Fucking shit made me sick. I didn't join the Red Wolves thirty fucking years ago just to be a fucking cunt in my golden years! But I couldn't talk anybody into getting rid of him. Oh no. Everybody *loves* North Tabion. Thinks he's the guy who's going to bring the Red Wolves into the future. Well, I've got something to say about it and damned if it didn't mean getting the Demon Devils involved. Then *you* showed up and saw me shaking hands with Gray Dog, a fucking witness. Fucking bitch!"

"If you'd have just let me use the phone, none of this would've happened," she cried.

"Shut up," he ordered.

He pushed her into the shack and pulled out another zip tie, which he looped through the ones already tied around her wrist before securing her to one of the bars that ran across the window.

"I may have a use for you, so you're going to stay here until I figure out how to salvage this fucking operation," he spat.

She flinched as spittle landed across her cheek.

"I've got one last shot at North and if I fail then you're going to be my consolation prize to the Demon Devils."

With that, he stormed out of the shack. Part of her was glad he was gone and that all he'd done was leave her tied up. It could've been much, much worse. On the other hand, he'd be back — or worse, he'd forget about her. She heard the van start up and drive away, the sound of the engine fading out as it left her behind. Alone. Tied to a window bar.

She was going to have to think of something fast. She didn't want to die here like this.

* * * *

When his stomach rumbled, Leo decided to pick up Merrie so they could go to lunch. He shut off the overhead light and headed to reception.

"Merrie, what do you — ?"

Unease settled over him when he discovered she wasn't at her desk.

"Merrie?"

He walked toward the hallway where the bathroom was located. He knocked on the closed door.

"Merrie?"

No answer.

Unease turned into worry and he turned back toward the reception. At the computer, he saw she'd been entering payments and making notations in the books of who had paid what and how much. The last scribbled word turned his blood cold.

Axe.

He ran to the back room to the camera equipment and scrolled through the recording until he saw a man walk in and raise a gun. His heart sank as he watched Merrie walk out the door with Axe keeping a gun trained on her. With shaking hands, he reached for his phone and dialed his brother.

"Lunch already?" Braden teased as he answered.

"Braden... He took her," Leo choked out. "He had a gun. She's gone."

"What?" Braden bit out. "How do you know?"

"I'm staring at the recording monitor. He's pointing a gun at her!"

"I'm on my way."

Leo hung up. He couldn't seem to take his eyes off the monitor or the terrified expression on Merrie's face as he replayed it over and over. He had been right there, right in the back, only a few doors away. He hadn't heard anything. And she'd been abducted by...by that mad man. Why the hell hadn't they taken precautions? Because he hadn't believed the man would be desperate enough to try something in broad daylight.

Fury coursed through him. Axe shouldn't have been loose. Givon assured them he was going to arrest that man, so how had he been able to kidnap Merrie?

Angrily, he dialed Givon's number.

"This is Sheriff—"

"He took her!" he shouted into the receiver. He was so upset he didn't know what to do. He wasn't the one who usually got upset. He'd always been the calm, collected one between him and Braden but right now, all he wanted to do was hit something—or reach through the phone and punch Givon's lights out.

"Leo? What are you—?"

"I'm staring at my video monitor watching Axe lead my girlfriend out the door at gunpoint, so what the fuck happened with arresting the son of a bitch?"

"Shit! I put an APB out on him and we've been searching for him everywhere."

"Searching? Well I fucking found him! He's on my security monitor!"

"I'm on my way."

"Yeah, that's what Braden said," Leo muttered, but he was already talking to the disconnected emptiness of a hang up.

* * * *

North checked his magazine then popped it back into his gun before sliding the piece back into its holster. He stalked out of his room in the clubhouse back into the main area that housed the bar, a pool table, old ratty couches and a huge flat-screen television where various members sat watching it. Two of his officers sat at the bar, his VP John Draven and Skids, who happened to be Axe's best friend.

He caught their attention and nodded for them to follow then he entered into church, waiting. A moment later, they came into the meeting room and he closed the door behind them.

"What's up?" Draven asked. When North had been voted in as president of the club, he'd quickly nominated Draven as his right hand. John Draven was a couple of years younger than Axe but North wanted young blood to lead the Red Wolves and bring the club into the future by becoming a legit. Draven had proven himself above and beyond loyal to the club.

"Axe turned traitor," he said, deciding blunt honesty was the best scenario.

"The hell you say," Skids growled.

He knew Skids was going to be defensive, so he picked his words carefully.

"It's true," he said. "He was seen shaking hands with Gray Dog and he almost killed the witness to hide his disloyalty."

"Fuck," Draven muttered. "Why? Why would he do that to the colors?"

North shook his head. "I don't know a hundred percent but he's been the most opposed with us getting out of the extortion business. Skids, has he said anything to you?"

"No," Skids said angrily. "Not a fucking word. Are you sure about this, North?"

"I am. I talked to the witness myself. That's why I gotta be sure about you, Skids. You and Axe are close."

Skids straightened his spine, threw his shoulders back. "My loyalty is to this club. If Axe violated that trust, then I'll be the first one to take him down."

North narrowed his eyes and studied the man. He saw only clear truth shining back and he slowly let out his breath. Dealing with one traitor was hard enough. He didn't want to think about dealing with two.

"All right," he said. "He's out there now but the sheriff has a warrant out for his arrest. We have to find him before the law does. This is a club matter."

"Agreed," Draven said.

"Yeah," Skids seconded.

"For now, let's keep this between us," North said. "We have too many guys who'll shoot first and I want the pleasure of kicking Axe's ass myself."

"Get in line," Skids snarled and stomped out of the room.

North and Draven shared a look and followed. They left the clubhouse, heading toward their bikes when the sound of a gunshot ricocheted over North's head. Flinching, North ducked and a searing pain sliced across his scalp as he fell backward. Blood poured down his face. People scrambled from all over, yelling and firing back at the unseen assailant. Skids threw himself over North, protecting him from any further attacks.

Fuck, my head hurts…

It was the last coherent thought he had before oblivion claimed him.

* * * *

As Givon raced out of the door, his cell phone went off. Impatiently he glanced at it and saw North's name.

"Get to Leo's office," he answered without waiting for North to greet him. "Axe took Merrie—"

"It's Draven, Sheriff."

Givon's blood turned cold and he came to a complete stop. His heart thundered in his chest. There was only one reason why Draven would be calling from North's phone. Not many knew how close they were and not many would know his nickname in North's contact list.

"What happened to him?" he asked quietly, steeling himself.

"Someone shot him. Skids and I are thinking it was Axe. We're at Destiny General right now."

Fuck! Givon had to choke down the bile that surged up from his gut. He really didn't want to ask this next question but he had to know. He forced himself not to react at all and, as best as he could, he asked the next question.

"Will he live?"

"Yeah, luckily it was just a deep scratch that needed some stitches," Draven answered.

Givon sagged in relief.

"But Axe split on us," Draven added, "and we have no idea where he is."

"Okay," Givon replied. "Stay with North. I'm on my way."

"You don't need to come. I called you 'cause I knew you'd want to know."

"And I appreciate that. But going after the president of the club is personal. Axe blindsided him so he might attack again. Tell North I'm on my way to pick him up."

Chapter Twenty-Two

As soon as Givon stepped out of his truck, Leo grabbed his shirt and punched him in the jaw. Givon flew back, hitting the side of his truck, hard. A tiny fraction of satisfaction coursed through him but his blood still burned with anger. Leo curled his hand again into a fist, and just as he went to charge someone's arms came around him from behind, trapping him, and North Tabion put himself between them.

"No, Leo," Braden said tightly. "This won't help anyone."

"It'll make me feel better," Leo snarled.

"He can arrest you for assaulting an officer," North reminded him.

"Then I better get in a few more punches and make it really worth locking my ass up."

"Stop it," Braden warned him. "We have to concentrate on Merrie."

Givon pushed himself away from his truck and stalked toward him, gently probing his bruised jaw.

"Are you through?" he asked Leo.

Leo wanted to punch him again, but Braden's arms were steel bands around him. Slowly, sanity returned. He gave a quick nod and Braden's eased up on his hold.

"What happened to you?" Leo asked North, pointing to the bandage around North's head.

"Axe took a shot at me."

"What?" Leo gasped. "Why is he after you?"

"Because if I get to him first, I'm putting a bullet in his fucking head," North replied coldly.

"I did *not* hear that," Givon grumbled.

"Did you see Merrie?" Braden asked.

"I didn't even see *him*. Luckily for me, the fucker is a lousy shot."

"I'd like to see your security recording," Givon said to Leo.

Leo turned to stomp back into the office, not bothering to check if Givon was following or not. Moments later, he crowded into the small room with the other men, watching the scene play out. The camera set angled from the corner of the waiting room, catching the front door and the reception desk. Axe was clearly seen coming in and pulling out a gun. The dialogue wasn't recorded but no words were really needed to see the terror on Merrie's face.

"Shit," Braden whispered.

"After our talk, I went looking for him all night," North said quietly. "Since the shooting, the club members are out hunting him as we speak. When they found out he's turned traitor then when he shot me… All they want is to get their hands on him."

"I don't really care about your motorcycle club," Leo said.

North glared at him.

"Where would Axe have taken Merrie?" Leo persisted.

North shook his head. "I don't know. We've checked all his haunts."

"Personal property?" Braden asked.

"He rents a room at the clubhouse," North answered.

"I've got all my deputies out searching and I can deputize a few other men," Givon said. "But this is a big county with lots of woods. I take it you guys want to come out on the hunt?"

Braden tapped Leo's arm. "One of us should stay behind, in case she comes back like she did the first time."

"I'll go mad if I stay here," Leo told him.

"How about we take turns looking?"

"Fine," Leo said. "But you're staying behind first."

He left of the small security room as the other men followed, although he didn't acknowledge them. When he walked back outside, Detective Christianson pulled up in his car.

"What's wrong? I got an urgent call from Sheriff Halloran."

"Axe took Merrie at gunpoint," Leo told him. He pointed at North. "And tried to kill him."

The detective paled. "When?"

"Half past eleven. I didn't realize it until about noon."

Leo opened his truck door, rummaged in the glove box then pulled out a map of the county and spread it out on the hood. "Okay, tell me where everyone is."

"I have Charlie scouting along Route 18, including the Devil's bar," Givon said. "Cynthia and George are patrolling the east and west."

"By the way," Braden asked Givon, "what happened to your department leak?"

"It would've been easy to fire the boy," Givon replied. "So I'm not going to make it easy."

"You could arrest him," Braden suggested.

"For running his mouth? I'd rather teach him a lesson."

North snorted. "Believe me. You don't want this ass riding yours. Poor bastard."

Givon smiled, cold and evil, giving Leo pause. Back when they were in high school, he remembered some kid smashing Givon's windshield with a baseball bat over some stupid thing or other. The next day, the kid had replaced the window himself while Givon had stood by watching. No one had ever figured out what had happened to make the guy fix what he'd broken, but damned if anyone ever messed with Givon Halloran again.

So Braden stayed behind while they all broke up and headed out searching. Leo hadn't a clue where to search, except where the Demon Devil's hung out, so he headed toward the bar where Deputy Charlie Earenflight was also patrolling.

He remembered the turf war that had raged when the Demon Devils settled into Destiny twenty years ago. Braden was off at college but he'd deferred his own schooling for two years to help Clip with the ranch. It had been a dangerous time, even to go into town for groceries. He hadn't thought highly of either motorcycle club. Things had settled down, especially when Old Patch had taken over the Red Wolves. But the animosity hadn't completely gone away.

He drove by the bar on Route 18 several times, hoping that he would see something—anything. The parking lot remained empty except for a couple of bikes. He passed Charlie a time or two and waved at the deputy.

Where would Axe take Merrie? Had he hurt her? Was she crying or suffering? The questions tormented him until he thought he'd go mad. He'd promised her she'd be safe. He'd told her that he and Braden would protect her.

God, he was a stupid fucking fool.

All he could do was pray that he'd get the opportunity to make it up to her. He couldn't live without her.

After a few hours of driving around, hoping to see Axe or Merrie, he went back to change places with Braden. When he walked into the house, silence greeted him. He experienced the crushing weight of one possible future—one where Merrie might never be back. It hit him so hard he sank to his knees. He let out a roar of pain, wincing when all it did was echo back.

* * * *

Twilight dusted the sky when Braden, Givon, North and the other two deputies arrived back at the house. Leo had every light turned on, thinking it was like a candle in the window, leading the lost back home.

As everyone piled into the living room, Leo saw the frustration on their faces. He turned toward the kitchen to find something to do—maybe brew some coffee—when the sheriff's phone buzzed.

"Yeah?" Givon barked. "What? Where? Holy shit. All right. We're on our way."

He hung up and turned.

"What?" Braden demanded.

"She's safe," Givon said.

Relief, sweet and sharp, rush through Leo.

"Where is she?" he asked.

Givon sighed, the only indication that something wasn't quite copasetic.

"Givon?"

"Seems like Gray Dog rescued her."

Absolute silence met his statement. Leo saw that even North was dumbstruck.

"Excuse me?" Braden demanded, breaking the disbelief in the room.

"She's at their bar on Route 18."

Without another word, Leo left—just walked right out of the door toward his truck. He slid behind the wheel just as Braden got into the passenger seat. The two glanced at each other and Leo knew he must look just as relieved as his brother did. Leo started up the truck and took off.

Chapter Twenty-Three

Evening had just broken over the land when Merrie heard an engine rumble up to the door. She'd tried all day to snap the zip ties holding her captive but the thick plastic was unbreakable. Due to her efforts to break free, she'd rubbed the skin around her left wrist raw and it bled slightly. After a while, she'd given up. It was either take a break or tear off her hand, and she wasn't ready to do that.

Tired of standing, she had to pee, plus hunger gnawed at her gut. But all those discomforts fled as she waited for Axe to come back inside. What would he do with her now? Panic wanted to take over her brain but she forced herself to stay calm. Composure allowed her to think and if there was a way to get out of this mess alive, she had to have her wits about her.

Axe didn't walk into the cabin right away. Footsteps reached her from outside as he walked around for a few minutes, skittering some rocks and cracking some branches. Then she heard another vehicle and her heart began to race. Maybe someone had figured out where she was! Maybe they were here to rescue her!

She strained her ears to listen.

"Did anyone follow you?" Axe demanded.

"What the hell did you do, Axe?" Detective Christianson demanded. Merrie frowned at the familiarity he seemed to have with her abductor.

"None of your goddamned business," Axe retorted. "I got North! I did it—"

"You got shit, Axe. You nicked him and now he's out hunting your ass."

"No! You lie!"

"Out of the two of us, who's the fucking douche bag? I assure you it's not me."

"Then you gotta help me," Axe pleaded. "You gotta—"

"I don't have to do shit. I knew this was going to be trouble the moment you called asking for my help."

"Yeah, for some dumb reason I thought you might actually be of use."

"I was lying low, trying to let all this fucking bullshit blow over. But no! You have to go shoot the Wolves' president and kidnap the girl."

"There's a warrant out for my arrest!" Axe shouted.

"I know!" Detective Christianson shouted back. "Where's the girl, Axe?"

"Does it matter?"

"Of course it fucking matters! I'm taking her back."

"You can't!" Axe protested. "She's my only hope now of getting out of this alive."

Merrie didn't hear anything for a moment and she could only imagine what was going on.

"Put the damn gun away," Axe snarled. "You're not going to kill your little brother."

Brother! Nausea churned in her belly.

"I'm no longer your brother," the detective said. "I'm a cop. And I'm here to arrest you and take the girl back."

"You wouldn't dare. DCI will be on your back faster than you can blink."

"I know. But I can't turn my back on this anymore. I'm still a cop and I still value my badge. I may have been buying myself time until retirement, but I have to do the right thing, regardless of you being blood. Now, where's the fucking girl?"

A moment later, the door opened and Detective Christianson swore as he put his gun back in its holster. He pulled out a Leatherman tool and flipped out the knife. He sawed through the zip tie, careful not to nick her. Finally freed, she rubbed her cut wrist as best as possible with the fingers of her other hand.

"Thank you," she whispered.

"I'm sorry for this," Detective Christianson told her with regret in his voice. "I knew my brother had fucked up but I thought time would just...wash it all away. I thought it'd blow over and you'd be safe again."

"Can you take me home? Or to the sheriff's station?"

He nodded. "Of course, I—"

"She ain't going anywhere!" Axe bit out as he came into the cabin.

Detective Christianson took a step toward his brother and as quick as lightning, Axe pulled a .38 pistol from behind his back. The detective held up his hands and Merrie did the same.

"Put the gun down," Christianson said. "You're not going to shoot me and turn this into an even worse situation."

"Fuck you," Axe snarled. "I ask for your fucking help and all you give me is shit. Never once in all my life have you ever helped me, Clark. Just this once, why couldn't you have been a decent brother? You take off and become a cop and you're *ashamed* of who I am?"

"Of course I'm ashamed. Look at you. You're pathetic. I've spent my whole career putting criminals like you behind bars. And you think I should be proud that my brother is a goddamn extortionist? A goddamn crook? Fuck you, *Andrew.*"

Axe fired the gun.

Merrie screamed and jumped back as blood splattered everything, including herself, the bullet hitting Detective Christianson directly in the chest. He gave one little gasp before crashing face first where blood rapidly pooled around him. Axe pointed the weapon in her direction. Merrie literally stared down the barrel of a smoking gun.

"Come on," Axe muttered. "I've got one last card to play."

Shaking, she did what he'd ordered. The last thing she wanted was to wind up like the poor detective, murdered in some small dingy hunter's cabin in the middle of nowhere.

He must have run out of zip ties. Instead of using them to tie her up, he used some bungee cords to twist around her arms and hook her to the interior of the van. If she didn't have the bulky cast on her right wrist, she might have been able to free herself, but as it was, she didn't have the strength to unhook the restraints.

They bounced along, and somehow, the ride didn't seem as long as the first time she'd been in the van. When it came to halt sometime later, he threw open the back and unhooked her. Then he grabbed her arm and dragged her forward. Only then did she recognize they were at the Demon Devil's bar.

Back where the nightmare had begun.

Two men watched them approach, both frowning. She read the word *prospect* on both their vests and realized that Axe was still wearing his with the red band around the bottom.

"What the fuck do you want?" asked one of the prospects.

"She's for Gray Dog," Axe snapped. "He'll want her. I'm joining the Demon Devils."

The two prospects looked at each other. One shrugged then gave Axe the nod to enter. The doors opened and Axe pushed her into the bar. Heavy metal played over the speakers and a layer of cigarette smoke hung low in the air. Every pair of eyes in the place observed her as she stumbled forward. The music abruptly cut off, leaving the room eerily quiet.

"What the ever-loving fuck is *this*?" Gray Dog snapped.

Axe shook her as if she were some kind of prize. "I brought her — to show my loyalty to the Demon Devils. I can still join your table and we can take over this county. Like I told you, I have Intel on the Wolves that can bring them down."

Gray Dog calmly walked around the bar and came to stand a few feet away from where Axe held her captive. He didn't look at her.

"My sanction for you to join us rested on you providing me with North Tabion's head," Gray Dog stated coldly. "But do you know who I got a call from earlier today? None other than that very same fucker who is looking for you. It seems like your shooting skills are lacking. So, Axe, I'm going to have to revoke my endorsement."

"You can't do that!" Axe all but screamed. "This bitch is who screwed up my plans and now I've corrected it. I'll kill her right now for you."

The cold barrel of Axe's gun pressed against the back of her head. She couldn't help the small whimper that escaped her. Terror churned in her stomach, making her wonder if she was about to upchuck and as much as she wanted to run away, her feet seemed frozen to the ground.

"That's all I need," Gray Dog sneered. "Her DNA splattered all over this fucking bar. There's too many people looking for her, numbnuts."

The gun wavered in his hand. Axe was losing control. "I've gone too far, Gray Dog. I can't go back to the Red Wolves. Not now. You owe me this."

"I don't owe you shit," Gray Dog muttered. "You came to me, remember? You asked me if there was any way a Red Wolf could join the Demon Devils. You even asked not to join as a fucking prospect. You wanted the glory and the badge, didn't you? Well, fuck you, Axe. My club, my rules. You're a Red Wolf in Demon Devil territory—a fucking traitor."

The next moment seemed to stretch into infinity. Merrie couldn't take her gaze off Gray Dog, who simply watched Axe over her shoulder. The stares of Demon Devils crawled over her skin like ants. This must be how they got their name. She certainly felt like she was standing in a pit of Hell.

Axe shifted he gun from the back to her head to over her shoulder. It barely registered in her brain that he now pointed the barrel at Gray Dog before the report of a gun filled the room, only it wasn't from *his* gun. She flinched instinctively then didn't move a muscle— not even when Axe's body fell back with a thud. From behind Gray Dog, a man held a gun, a man with long dark hair and a snake tattoo on his arm—the same man from her car, the one who had been driving. She wondered, in a detached sort of way, if he was going to shoot her next. Would it have been better never to see it coming or to face the bullet head on?

Although she tried to keep herself as still as possible, shivers suddenly gripped her. Gray Dog slowly walked up to her.

"Now what shall I do with you?" he asked softly.

A million ideas ran through her mind, but the only thing that stuck was the realization she was going to have to say something meaningful to him if she hoped he'd spare her life. She looked around the room. Cold blank stares met her.

"I think," she began, but her mouth was so dry she had difficulty forming words. She swallowed as much saliva as she could find in her mouth and tried again. "I think you found me and rescued me."

Gray Dog cocked his head. "Come again?"

"You said too many people are looking for me," she answered steadily, using his own words against him. If she had to play on his vanity to save her neck, so be it. "And Axe has proved himself a traitor to the Red Wolves, which means he would have definitely become a traitor to the Demon Devils. When he took me captive to save his own neck, you realized just how bad a man he was, a liar to his colors and a liar to yours. So, you rescued me. And the media labels you a hero."

Gray Dog sucked in a deep breath and crossed his arms. "A hero, huh? And you being in my bar?"

"I was never in your bar," she said, keeping her gaze trained on him.

"And Axe being shot?"

"I never saw that happen," she stated firmly. "I was tied up in the back of his van. Blindfolded. The next thing I knew, you untied me and I have no idea where Axe went."

The shooter, who had stood behind Gray Dog, murmured something in his ear. Gray Dog gave a small smile, never taking his eyes from her. The man backed away but didn't go too far.

"I like being called a hero," Gray Dog said. "Most people in Destiny would label me the antichrist, so being a hero would give them a big old 'fuck you'. And now there's too many roads leading you back to my doorstep, so you better stick to that story, Miss Walden, and I do believe we have ourselves a deal."

She didn't say anything, just stood still and didn't look around. The less she saw, the better.

Gray Dog abruptly lost his smile and took a threatening step toward her. "But if you ever breathe one word about what happened here, we'll have business to take care of. Understand?"

"Yes," she said firmly. Boy did she understand. His meaning was coming through loud and crystal clear. "All I've ever wanted to do was put this...episode...behind me. I've no wish to go down memory lane."

Gray Dog relaxed. "Very well. Then it seems I have a phone call to make and a newspaper reporter to get ready for, plus smile for the camera. My man Gunner will wait with you outside."

The shooter, aptly named Gunner, strode forward and took her arm. She didn't look down as he steered her to the door. She had no wish to see Axe's lifeless body. And she absolutely had no desire ever to see the inside of the Demon Devil's bar again.

Chapter Twenty-Four

Merrie wasn't sure what was going to happen. She waited in the parking lot of the Demon Devil's bar, shivering a little from the cool night air. Gunner stood next to her. He hadn't said a word to her in the whole time they'd been there. She'd turned her back when several of the bikers had brought out Axe's body. Soon, she heard the van take off and a few minutes after that, the newspaper reporter showed up.

Gray Dog came out to stand next to her as the reporter interviewed her, forcing her to talk about her ordeal. She changed things just enough to make it sound like the Demon Devils were the heroes of this nightmare, Gray Dog in particular. He'd rescued her, saved her from a madman, who had thought he could become part of their organization.

"I was only doing what anybody would have done," Gray Dog stated as the camera pushed close to his face. "For so long, people have this warped view of who and what a motorcycle club actually consists of. We are law-abiding, a society of caring people. It was not only my pleasure to save Miss Walden, but it was also my duty from one human being to the other."

For the most part, Merrie let Gray Dog do all the talking, only nodding and agreeing with whatever the reporter wanted her to confirm. Minutes into the interview, she saw Leo's truck approaching on the road. Her heart jumped and everything blurred as she left the reporter and Gray Dog behind to run toward her two men.

The truck screeched to a halt and Braden bailed out of it. He ran to her, throwing his arms around her and engulfing her in a warm, tight embrace. Behind her, Leo curved his big body to her back, and just like that, everything in her world righted itself. She didn't care about anything else, not how Gray Dog was becoming a hero in the eyes of the world, not how Axe's body was probably going to disappear, and certainly not the secrets she was now forced to keep. She'd do it all and more to be safe, and more importantly, to keep her family safe. She'd come from a hard life and she wasn't going to let one more dark blight in the past destroy her future. It was over.

The next few hours were devoted to answering questions and repeating the lie that Gray Dog saved her. He had told the reporter that Axe had brought her to his club in hopes of being an incentive to accept him into the ranks of the Demon Devils. Gray Dog flat out said he knew something was wrong and that he had to rescue her. When he'd declined Axe's request, he said that Axe had grabbed Merrie to take her, but he'd fought him and managed to get Merrie away. After that, Axe had fled and they had no idea where he'd gone.

Givon asked to inspect the bar, which Gray Dog happily complied with. Merrie wondered what the bikers had done to clean up the interior but she quickly let that thought die. From now on, she couldn't think of those things, couldn't allow herself to wonder and contemplate the 'what ifs'. Gray Dog caught her eye and the look he gave her more than reinforced her need to keep her mouth shut. She gave him the barest nod then turned away. She'd uphold her end of the bargain and she'd quickly throw away the memories that went with it.

She told the deputies about the hunting cabin and what had happened to Detective Christianson, as well as his family connection to Axe, but apologized when she couldn't tell them the cabin's location since the back of the van hadn't had any windows. Finally, the long night ended and Leo helped her into the truck, placing her between him and Braden.

Every light shone in the house but she didn't care. She might even need to sleep with the lights on for a few days, just until the terror faded from her mind. Tears poured from her eyes as relief flooded through her. So much had been drained from her that dizziness assailed her.

She was safe.

It was over.

Axe would never hurt her again.

Although she couldn't ever say that statement aloud, it was enough just knowing justice had been served. It might not be civilized justice, but perhaps that was for the best. There wouldn't be a trial, she wouldn't have to relive the terror and she'd never have to dread the idea of Axe being paroled.

Braden swept her up in his arms and carried her to the bathroom, where he and Leo turned on the shower and stripped her. Leo kept his body against the sting of the hot water while Braden pressed in behind her.

She had to keep her cast dry, so she turned to hang her wrist through the curtain.

Braden couldn't seem to stop touching her—her face, her hair, her neck, her shoulders. It was as though he couldn't get enough confirmation that she was there and safe. It would be a while until she was truly fine, but for now, being okay was good enough.

"What really happened?" Leo whispered into her ear. He rested his cheek on top of her head.

"What do you mean?"

"Honey, the Demon Devils don't do anything that doesn't put something in their pocket," Braden said. "Gray Dog wouldn't have *rescued* you, not unless he'd been promised something."

She didn't say anything, unwilling to lie to them, but at the same time, Gray Dog's words screamed through her head.

"Merrie?"

She smiled up at Braden. "I don't know—"

"Don't lie," Leo said.

"I have to," she replied.

"Why?"

She didn't want to say it. She wanted to forget it.

But Braden and Leo wouldn't let her.

"Always tell us the truth, sweetheart," Leo said.

"I need to protect you," she whispered.

Braden grasped her chin and lifted her head. "How about we protect each other? Whatever happened, we'll protect your secrets."

She nodded. "Let's get out of the shower first."

They quickly washed and dried off. Only when Merrie wore her sleep shirt and lay tucked in between Braden and Leo in bed did she tell them about her abduction. From beginning to end, everything poured out, even the threats Axe had used against her. When she got to the part where she had been standing in the Demon Devil's bar, she stumbled a bit. To say the words aloud would make it real and she didn't know if she wanted to relive it. But they both took hold of one of her hands and held tight, then her words just poured out.

"He pulled the gun on Gray Dog then...he was dead. A man named Gunner shot him, and he was the same guy who was driving my car that night I jumped from it. I recognized the tattoo on his arm."

"What happened to Axe?" Leo asked.

"I don't know," she replied. "I really have no idea what happened to the body and I don't care to know. But Gray Dog was wondering what to do with me and I had to think of something. I didn't want to die, so I persuaded him to be my hero."

"That explains the newspaper," Leo replied. "North's going to love that."

The sarcastic tone suggested anything but. Not that she gave a shit. The only things Merrie cared about were the two men sitting next to her.

"He said as long as I hold my silence, we have a deal. If I tell anyone...the deal's off."

"Okay," Braden said. "Then this doesn't go any farther than this room. Agreed?"

"Agreed," Leo said.

Merrie nodded. "Agreed."

Braden kissed her softly on the lips. "Listen, Merrie, I know we haven't known each other long and I know I've been a colossal prick for some of that time. But I more than care for you, Merrie. I...I'd like for you to stay, to see if we can build a future."

"Oh, Braden. I more than care for you too."

Leo turned her head toward him. "Will you stay with us, Merrie? Will you see if we can have a future together?"

"Yes!" she exclaimed. "Of course, yes. As long as sharing never becomes an issue between us. I'd never want to be the thing that separates you two."

Leo smiled tenderly. "Braden and I promise to never let that happen."

"Yeah," Braden said. "Any issues that arise, we talk about it together. I've learned my lesson."

"Good." She softened the word with a giggle. "I won't be afraid to crack my whip."

"I love your strength and your courage and I can't imagine going through life without you," Leo shared with her.

Merrie smiled. "You've both given me the thing I wanted most — a family. And I love you both for it."

Braden and Leo used actions to express their love. Leo trailed his hand up her leg, pushing her T-shirt as he went, touching her inner thigh and gently reaching higher until he realized she wasn't wearing panties. His gaze flew to hers and he offered her such a sexy, wicked grin that wetness instantly flooded her pussy. He explored her folds, coating his digits in her juice before dipping inside her. As he explored her with his talented fingers, Braden engulfed her sensitive nipples with his mouth. Merrie arched, wanting more.

Leo began a rhythmic thrusting that, combined with Braden caressing her breasts with his mouth and hands, soon had her panting and begging for release. Pleasure built and built until she couldn't help but succumb. She cried out as the orgasm crashed over her and she rode the waves that Leo and Braden had wrung from her. When she stopped shuddering, Leo withdrew his fingers and proceeded to lick her cream off them.

Braden quickly slipped off his boxer briefs and his thick cock sprang up. He straddled her, being careful not to sit on her, and let his dick rest between her breasts.

"Merrie," he murmured sexily. "Lick my cock."

He began lightly thrusting and she did her best to push her tits together to provide a snug channel for him to burrow through. Each time he pushed up, she'd flick her tongue over him, delving into the hole. He groaned deeply, the sound turning her on. Knowing she gave him such pleasure heightened her arousal even more.

Leo spread her legs then buried his face between her thighs. He flicked her clit with his tongue before pushing it into her clenching channel. Over and over he played with her, teasing her lightly enough to keep her motor revved but not enough to trip her orgasm. Braden pulled back first, easing from between her breasts and off her chest to open Leo's nightstand. He grabbed two condoms and a bottle of lube. Seeing it, excitement shot through her. *Oh yes, yes, yes, yes!* This was what she wanted, what she needed—her two men buried deep inside her body. Taking her. Claiming her.

When Leo rose from her pussy, she all but salivated for both their cocks. This time Leo slid home in her cunt and Braden teased her back entrance. Braden lubed her up, stretched her with a finger then two. He withdrew his fingers and just before the burn eased, he possessed her in one thrust. His cock filled her. Pain mixed with pleasure then faded into raw rapture. She floated in heaven as Leo and Braden pumped into her body, sending her higher and higher into orbit.

Her orgasm crested over her and she cried out loudly as she bucked wildly between them. Her pussy muscles squeezed and contracted around Leo's cock, but her back hole also clenched tightly, sending both men over the precipice.

Later, they lay together in the darkness of the room, Merrie between them. She felt wanted, protected, and most importantly, loved. She'd finally found her place to belong.

Epilogue

This time around, Givon arrived second to the clearing. North watched behind his mirrored sunglasses as the sheriff pulled to a stop behind his beat-up truck. He scratched at the healing scab in his hairline, the bandage around his head now replaced with his usual American flag bandana. Givon jumped out from behind the steering wheel.

"What's this fucking bullshit about Gray Dog being a hero?" North instantly demanded.

"I don't know," Givon answered. "Merrie Walden is sticking with the story."

North snorted. "He threatened her, then."

"If he did, I can't do much about it unless she tells me the truth."

"Well, shit," North said. "We've had several businesses wanting the Demon Devils as their protectors instead of us. This is bad for the Wolves, Givon."

"You're going legit, North. I don't need to hear about your extracurricular extortion activities."

North chuckled. "There's a reason why the Red Wolves are just over the county line. Your reputation is safe, Sheriff."

"Fuck you, North," Givon grumbled. "You're still trouble in Destiny."

"So what's the deal between the three of them?" North asked.

"Who? Braden, Leo and Merrie?"

North nodded.

Givon shrugged. "They're together."

"Like...*all* together?"

"Well, I think it's more a case of the two men share her," Givon said.

"I don't know..." North shook his head. "I can't imagine sharing a woman in a long-term relationship. A one-night stand, sure, but no woman is worth being in bed with another man's junk for the long haul."

"Well," Givon replied. "It's not really our concern. But if it works for 'em? Hell, more power to them."

"I guess. Hey, want to go fishing soon? I haven't been to the lake since Old Patch died."

"That would be great," Givon said with a nod. "I could use a little break. Axe is going to remain an open case on my books since I can't list him as dead, although I'm pretty positive we never have to worry about him again."

"Yeah, that's a sure bet."

"Well, I better get back," Givon stated. "Let's get to that fishing trip soon, all right?"

"You betcha. Later, asshole."

"Jerk," Givon teased back.

About the Author

I like writing about the very ordinary girl thrust into extraordinary circumstances, so my heroines will probably never be lawyers, doctors or corporate high rollers. I try to write characters who aren't cookie cutters and push myself to write complicated situations that I have no idea how to resolve, forcing me to think outside the box. I love writing characters who are real, complex and full of flaws, heroes and heroines who find redemption through love.

I've been pretty fortunate in life to experience some amazing things. I've lived in France, traveled throughout Europe, Australia and New Zealand. I am a mom to an amazing little boy. I'm surrounded by friends and family. And although I love holding a book in my hand, I absolutely adore my ereader, which I've named Ruby. I love to hear from readers so I've made it really easy to find me on the web.

Beth D. Carter loves to hear from readers. You can find her contact information, website details and author profile page at http://www.totallybound.com.

Totally Bound Publishing